Be
Careless

JULIA DOGGART

CRAFTED
ESSENCE
PUBLISHING

To our younger selves

ACKNOWLEDGMENTS

With thanks to all those who crossed my path and
made life richer, whether that meeting was easy or hard.

1

Morgan saw the sign several seconds too late. He wrenched the wheel of his truck and spun into the dusty parking lot where he landed nose-to-nose with a split-rail fence. As he cut the engine and reached forward to pat the dash, he wished Tom had been there to witness his precision. His brother, who swapped cars like he swapped women, had always underestimated his old truck. She was rusty, sure, but every bit as good as the rentals lined up next to him like shiny new toys.

The cars alone convinced him that he didn't belong. It was bad enough that Kim had dumped him, but to sign him up for a life-writing retreat was pure passive aggression. He wished again that he had never mentioned it to his boss at the magazine. It was Zoe, never one to miss a chance, who had turned the poisoned gift into a writing job. Retreats were on trend; he must bite the bullet and give her a feature in under two thousand words.

Morgan sighed and stared out through his cracked windscreen towards an old yellow caravan half-hidden by a stand of trees. From a distance, the tires on the caravan looked flat and ribbons of paint danced off the sides like abandoned streamers. Yet the splash of color summoned a memory of the day his sister brought a canary home from school. Convinced that the bird was being held against its will, Faith had released it into the garden. Two days later, they had found the creature's stiff, unyielding body under the kitchen window; it had died trying to get back inside.

A burst of laughter from the far end of the parking lot drew his gaze back towards a cluster of men in tank tops with action-figure arms. He watched as they tossed bags into the trunks of cars like candy; their women, bright like spandex trumpet vine, laughed and offered applause; then, two-by-two, the couples got into their vehicles and sped away. When the dust settled, a single lone figure remained in view standing at the bottom of a set of steps.

Forced into action, Morgan raised his hand as if in greeting but really to stop the woman in her tracks. She paused, one foot on the lowest step, while a chorus line of peace flags stirred overhead.

Keeping her in his line of vision, Morgan brushed damp hair off his forehead, adjusted his ponytail and cranked open the driver's-side door. He flung his bags onto the ground, took a deep breath and stepped out from behind the safety of metal and glass.

The sensation, if he had to describe it, was of dropping down into his gut. He leaned back against the warm body of the truck and closed his eyes. He longed for a cigarette, but he'd finished his last pack on the deck of the ferry and he'd promised himself it would be his last.

The woman coughed and Morgan pushed himself upright. He slung both his bags over one shoulder and walked the fence-line to the top of the steps. As he loomed above her, the woman craned her neck and shielded her eyes from the sun.

"Welcome," she said. "You seemed lost in thought; I didn't like to disturb you."

Morgan took the steps two-at-a-time and received the woman's outstretched hand. Her fingers were feather-light and seemed to dance in his palm. He tried to remember

2

her name from the information packet. Dana? Or, was it Gina? He settled on the latter in his mind.

"We didn't expect you until later. The previous people have only just left. It's fine because no one used your cabin. They were a tantric yoga group and quite particular in their needs."

"Me too," said Morgan. "It was Doritos for lunch on the ferry."

She laughed at that and gestured for him to follow her. They moved, single-file, along a narrow path that led to a courtyard framed by buildings on two sides. At the far end, a thick weave of wisteria had wound up a supporting pillar and fanned out along a wooden arch. Pendulous blooms. He'd used that phrase once in a story when a city official had rambled on about the wisteria that covered the front of his home. He'd wanted to imply that the plant had more substance than the man. Zoe had guessed his intention, of course, but she let the line stand.

"There's the kitchen," Gina said, pointing to a closed door. "You can use it any time and it's always stocked with the basics. The meals are vegetarian, of course, but there's a deli in town if you crave meat. No one minds as long as you store it carefully in the communal fridge."

"I think I can survive ten days without meat," Morgan said, wondering if it was a lie.

They left the courtyard and followed a path set between bamboo and manicured rock garden. Wood chips, laid fresh that morning, made him stumble under the uneven weight of his bags. As he lost and found his footing, he kicked up a scent reminiscent of his father's workshop back home. He was about to tell Gina when she stopped abruptly at a small bridge.

"This is the alder marsh," she announced. "We consider it the heart or belly of this place."

Morgan peered into the murky water and caught the outline of iridescent plants hunkered down among the long-limbed alders. Trapped between the stagnant air of the marsh and a cocoon of overhead canopy, he felt immense pressure at his temples and willed Gina to move on. They crossed the bridge in silence and stopped again outside a simple cabin whose sign read: Owl's Nest.

"It's perfect," he whispered.

"We thought you'd like it," Gina smiled. "Dinner is at six followed by the first group gathering. If you have any questions, you can always find me in the office."

Morgan stayed on the porch and watched her leave, already protective of the cabin's dark interior. If she felt his gaze, Gina gave no sign; her steps were firm and confident, and her hips swayed in a figure-of-eight motion as if some internal rhythm had her in its grip. He watched until the trees and the marsh swallowed her up and then he tried the door of his cabin.

The wood, swollen from a wet winter, resisted his efforts at first and he was forced to use his shoulder. Once inside, he found the air musty but cool. He dropped his bags and tested the narrow bed with both hands. When the mattress gave under his probing fingers, he slumped down with relief then kicked off his boots and peeled away socks worn for too many days. He lay full length on the bed, and within moments, surrendered to the dips and valleys made by previous sleepers.

Above him, the roof sloped protectively onto thick logs that made him think again of his father. A man of hard, practical skills with an engineer's brain, John Anderson would have appreciated this cabin, but only after he'd inspected every corner, every joist, every instance of tongue and groove. He would have judged the place entirely by the skill revealed in its construction.

What was it Kim had said? Kim, who worked in advertising and reduced everything to copy: *Your father is solid stock, but you're a poorly conceived brand.* She'd said it with contempt, had meant her words to sting, but something in the phrase had made him laugh. Soon, they were both laughing, doubled over and repeating her words as if they formed a private joke between them.

But that day marked a change; Kim began her calculated retreat. Small things at first: more time at the old apartment, less time looking for a tenant; a slow but steady trickle of possessions away from their shared space. Most noticeable of all, she relaxed her scrutiny of his inner world. And he had let it happen; in fact, he welcomed the slide into a more casual way of relating.

The final nail in the coffin - he tended to reminisce in clichés – had been a tiresome conversation about the possibility of kids. When he didn't respond fast enough, Kim shouted and waved her hands in his face like flies.

"It wasn't just a hesitation," she'd screamed. "It was a declaration."

He'd backtracked of course, tied himself in knots, tried to smooth it all over.

"I can un-hesitate. Look, here I am unhesitating. Kids with you would be..."

And then he did it again - hesitated. Kim had just stared at him.

"Kids would be… a miracle; exciting; fun; unbelievable. Take your pick."

"Unbelievable – that's the one."

A week later, she had packed her remaining possessions and left. There were no more tears, no overt anger, just an eerie compassion that manifested in gentle speech and soft touches to his arm or elbow when he got in her way.

For a while after she left, he was certain she would return. But as the days crawled past and turned to weeks, his confidence faltered and then died when he saw her out at a restaurant with another man.

The notice of her engagement followed some months after that. A white card with dark, malevolent text landed in his mailbox: the parents of blah blah blah request the presence of blah blah blah at some pretentious location. Morgan ripped up the card and crammed the pieces into his crusty toilet. It took three flushes to wash them away.

In the same envelope, discovered much later that evening, he found the brochure for the life writing retreat and a brief note in Kim's hand: 'You're in! Hope it helps.' Like some twisted consolation prize: Sorry I left. Sorry I moved on and chose someone better. But here, it might help to write it all down.

So that was that. Kim was never coming back and Morgan would no longer be her personal source of either joy or disappointment. Well, she could go to hell. They all could – Kim, the new man, his parents with their 'told you so' attitude, perfect Tom, even Faith who was 'concerned' about his emotional well-being.

Morgan turned on his side and pulled knees to chest as the cabin walls drew closer. His thoughts, speeding for weeks, stopped abruptly; he pictured a cartoon pile-up of cerebral bytes jammed against each other on the mind's freeway and gasping for breath. Another huge intake of air and its release, and then he gave way to an underlying tiredness that was unassailable and dense. He lay there, a pile of abandoned bones with no idea how he might reassemble.

2

A late afternoon chill crept across the marsh and settled, uninvited, into Morgan's bones. He rolled onto his back, stretched like a crumpled starfish and swung bare feet onto chilly floorboards. His upper body felt immobile, as if his neck and shoulders had been injected with cement.

Blurry with sleep, he inspected the doll-house furniture around him: compact wooden desk, school-room chair, half-empty bookshelf and basin just large enough for hands. Above the desk, a framed photograph showed an owl caught mid-dive, its wings unfurled and eyes fixed like marbles; whatever it hunted was out of the frame.

Two strides took him to the basin where the cold tap was stubborn and the water tainted by rust. When it ran clear, he splashed his face and neck and then scrubbed at his hands with a nub of dried soap. Despite the scrubbing, his nails remained black from a recent oil change on the truck; he wondered if Gina had noticed.

Above the sink, an oval mirror hung like a clouded moon and reflected a face as pale as his mother's best china. Morgan's hair, held back by string for the drive, had worked loose and formed into shoulder-length matted tangles.

He kneaded the knots with his fingers and then dried his hands on a towel washed so many times it felt like pumice. His socks, thrown near the sink, were wet from his earlier splashing; a search in his bag produced only a mismatched pair - one brown sock and one blue. He laced his boots and hoped that no one would notice. On the surface, at least, he was ready to meet the group.

Morgan retraced the route he had taken with Gina and found the courtyard empty as before. But voices drifted down to him from upstairs windows, and he had the sensation of being watched. He ducked into the kitchen where a middle-aged woman in a blue bandana was elbow-deep in salad.

"I'm making tofu enchiladas as well," she told him, and smiled sympathetically when Morgan failed to repress a shudder. "There's bread in that tin and cheese in the fridge," she said. "Knock yourself out."

He cut two thick slabs of bread and doused them with mustard before adding slabs of cheese. Then he brewed coffee and watched as the woman smeared her enchilada filling onto tortillas and bundled them into submission. She showed the same skill he'd observed in Faith when he watched her swaddle her twins.

Unwilling to engage in small talk, Morgan took coffee and sandwich into the garden and perched on the edge of a raised vegetable bed that was set against the slope of a runaway lawn. The air seemed thick with lavender and the music of bees; every so often, a hummingbird thrummed past on its route between feeders and left a flash of glory. It certainly wasn't the worst place to be trapped for the next ten days.

Five minutes before the first scheduled session, he checked the contents of his green canvas bag: notebook, laptop, thesaurus and assorted pens. The bag had held up well over two decades of near-constant use which dated back to the day he had taken it from his father's workshop without permission. At the time, he had braced for any repercussions, but there hadn't been so much as a glance of disappointment from his father's watery Anglo eyes. Father and son acted as if Morgan was, and always had been, the legitimate owner of the bag.

Down in the meadow, he approached the octagonal wooden building that perched like a rotund Tardis on the flattened grass. There were bodies inside, visible yet remote through the floor-to-ceiling glass. He peered into a narrow vestibule, but an ordered line of shoes made him recoil, and he almost collided with Gina.

"I'm about to sound the gong," she told him. "Are you running away?"

The gong, big as a dinner tray, hung from a branch above their heads. Morgan took the mallet from Gina's hand and struck the gong three times, letting the sound spread and diminish. Gina nodded her approval, and he followed her inside. As he unlaced his boots, he accepted what the shoes had made clear: he would be the only man in a sea of women.

"Don't worry," Gina assured him, as if she could read his mind, "Gill's a great facilitator; he'll make you feel at home."

"He?" echoed Morgan, weak with relief.

In his head, Gill, soft G, had been a woman; but Gill, hard G, had turned out to be a man. He picked up one of the books Gina had piled on a table near the door and studied the dust-jacket; a young man in a turtleneck with impossibly smooth skin stared back.

The blurb was effusive: 'A gem of a memoir that bursts out of the closet with tenderness and wit.' Since then, there had been two non-fiction volumes on writing and a novel. Not a bad haul.

Morgan set the book back down and advanced into the room. A dozen or more women were talking in pairs and none of them looked up at his arrival. Marooned in the midst of female voices, he tacked towards a circle of low-lying chairs and forced his limbs into a cross-legged position. As his heart signaled like a ship's horn on a foggy morning, he measured the distance between himself and the door.

A chime rose above the chatter and the women muted and then drifted towards their seats like seeds. All except one. This body, wrapped in a dream-coat of shawls, hovered and delayed as if needing an audience even for this one small act.

"You're brave to be here," a woman said, leaning towards Morgan.

Her face was devoid of make-up, and her lips vanished when she smiled as if worn out by kindness.

"Brave? Honey, he's lucky. The cock in the proverbial henhouse."

Laughter crashed through the circle like a pinball then died away. The accent was southern, Georgia or Tennessee perhaps, and belonged to the woman with the shawls. Her face, pale except for a slash of red on the pouting mouth and a heavy rim of eye liner, was framed by long bottle-blonde curls.

An art piece, Morgan thought, a living installation. The woman laughed again, as if hurling a lasso across the circle. A second chime thinned her laughter. A third, echoing from a palm-sized metal bowl, reduced the room to silence.

"Welcome," said a tall man, whose angular face seemed tight as a drum. "My name is Gill. We have a lot to cover. We want to get you writing, but we want to get you writing well. What do I mean by that? What is 'good' writing? Any thoughts?"

Gill's head swiveled, owl-like, and he gazed at them with hazel eyes magnified by thick corrective lenses; the dust jacket photo was several decades old. Most of the women avoided his stare, but a few dared answers. Gill either corrected or refined their words. Then, having exposed their ignorance, he proposed further introductions to break the ice.

"We want to know who you are and why you came. Keep it brief - a scene rather than a chapter - and describe the object you brought. I'll start and then we'll go clockwise around the circle."

Gill levered himself up from his deck chair, higher than a BackJack but still an operational challenge, and placed a large wooden bowl into the center of the circle. He drew a pen from his breast pocket and squinted along the shaft.

"This fountain pen belonged to my father," Gill told them. "Each morning, he made hand-written notes about the weather. It symbolizes dedication to a task."

Gill placed the pen into the bowl and caused a ripple of movement among the women as they searched bags and worried objects as if they were prayer beads. Morgan made a mental inventory of the contents of his pockets. He also wondered if Gill's father was dead, or if his son had wrested the pen from him in an act of filial succession.

Next to speak was Andrea, a woman in her forties with the face of a startled child. She leaned forward, revealing knee-high white socks under khaki trousers, and placed a glass bead into the bowl. She said beads strung together were more than the sum of their parts.

A wave of introductions followed, and the tide moved inexorably towards Morgan until it hit the bulwark of the women with the shawls.

"Hello y'all," she said. "My name is Savannah."

She spoke as if on a stage; her story was a grab-bag of signs and omens that had led to Gill's door.

"And your object?" Gill prompted.

She flourished a laminated card that she used as a fan before setting it down on top of the bowl.

"My top ten musings," she explained. "First: The muse is no one's mistress. Second: If at first you don't amuse, then muse, muse, and muse again. Third..."

"We get the picture," Gill interrupted, "but what does this tell us about you?"

Careless, thought Morgan, since her card obscured the other offerings.

"Fearless," said Savannah. "I'm not afraid to shine my light and claim my power."

"Thank you," Gill said. "On to the next."

Stories and objects followed. Morgan's favorite was a book-sized water-color showing a woman half-emerged from a shell. It came from Robin, the woman with the vanishing lips, and caused a murmur of appreciation around the circle.

"I used to be a minister," Robin explained, "and everything I did revolved around Sunday sermons. Last year, I quit the ministry. I gave up sermons for art."

Morgan almost applauded. His tongue had ridden up to the roof of his mouth, and he missed what the next woman said. Now it was his neighbor's turn. Lily had survived Nova Scotia winters and a bitter divorce. She offered a rusted piece of iron to symbolize her heart and hoped the workshop would galvanize new beginnings. Morgan swallowed hard and wiped sweaty palms on beleaguered thighs.

"Hello. My name is Morgan, and … I'm a man," he said, to a ripple of laughter. "I'm a features' writer at a magazine. I'm here on assignment and…because my ex-girlfriend signed me up."

The waiting faces had made him come clean. No need to add that Kim had moved on with her life guilt-free like a ship off-loading its anchor.

"I'm not exactly sure what I will get out of this," he added. "The object I brought is this stone."

It was a stone he had picked up that afternoon somewhere between the bridge and his cabin. He hadn't remembered putting it into his pocket.

"What does the stone represent?" Gill asked.

"It has a hole in it."

"A hole signifies emptiness," Gill persisted, "but it could also represent the potential for something new - a space of possibility."

"The space before invention," Morgan said, holding the stone up to his eye.

He tossed it towards the bowl, but the stone bounced off Savannah's card and Morgan was forced to crawl forward, head down, and remedy his error. Abject before the master, he had never felt so small.

3

'Spring-time in the Pacific Northwest. The inch of bud and leaf; the yawn of tensile pines; the surge of febrile undergrowth...'.

Pretentious crap. Morgan glanced at the delete button but hit save instead: 'draft seven'. Life might be surging, but he felt severed from its beat. Sleep had been elusive; it was too dammed quiet on this island. Gill had told them to just write and trust that a story would emerge. But what story? A childhood in rural Wisconsin felt achingly dull. So dull, that he'd escaped to Seattle. Well, almost Seattle; Tacoma was as close as he could afford.

If he was honest, city life had not been the stuff of headlines either. Feature-writing at a mid-level magazine meant seeing humanity at its self-indulgent worst. To date, he had feigned interest in hobbies that included geriatric Pilates, double-blind wine tasting, yoga with goats, and climbing walls while trussed like a chicken. His ambition, much like his gym membership, had faded after the first six months.

Morgan closed his laptop with a sigh and pulled his hair into a tighter ponytail, securing it with the rubber band he had worn on his wrist for months. He was supposed to ping the band whenever he wanted a smoke, but all it had done was reveal the frequency of his cravings. Maybe he should write about that – how craving became habit and how the absence of habit felt like a black hole.

Losing Kim had made things worse, like losing his will power. It was Kim who had instigated early morning runs, curated movie and museum visits, conversed about feelings. Without her, his days felt flabby and pointless. He wondered again why they had argued about babies that did not even exist.

As Morgan paced his cabin, the mirror sent angled shots of sunken cheeks and two-day stubble. It had been Kim who had stitched together home, work, family and the larger world. If it had felt like a tightrope at times – him scampering across with no dignity, trying to keep her happy – this alternative of a rope devoid of tension felt infinitely worse.

"You look like a drug addict," his mother had said, when he travelled home after the split, puffy with insomnia. "No one likes self-pity."

She'd been right, of course; he'd felt victimized by Kim's departure. She had delivered an act of severance that deftly disabled his life. Closer scrutiny might have revealed loneliness, or even need, but Morgan dismissed such rumblings in the tone his mother used to kill nascent signs of moral weakness. *Get a grip*, he said out loud, and reached for his jacket.

The world outside his cabin was drenched with rain and droplets seeped from the trees like simple blessings. He stopped at the bridge and admired the bubbles that had formed on the surface of the marsh. He stretched out a foot, seeking purchase on one of the logs, but it subsided with barely a struggle. It was proof; life was always in the process of dissolution or becoming.

If only his family understood. Faith had accused him of letting the relationship die. He'd pictured tubes, the kiss of life, a blood transfusion and wondered aloud what in truth he could have done differently. When Faith promised to hook him up with one of her friends, he'd felt a flash of hope. But he hadn't heard from her in weeks, and the only recent message on his phone had come from Kim who was checking on her investment. With this macabre thought, he left the bridge and continued on his way.

When Morgan arrived in the kitchen, it was occupied. A flock of women obscured his view of the toaster and complicated his path to the fridge. Still, he managed to slice open a cold bagel and then retrieve a stash of peanut butter and jelly from the fridge. As he closed the fridge door, Savannah loomed in front of him holding a peeled banana in one hand.

"Quite the gourmet," she commented, as she clamped painted lips around the shaft.

He ducked past her and hurried down to the gathering space where he sat as far as possible from Gill's chair. When the session began, he kept his head lowered and tried to focus his attention on the shares. There were concerns over poor sleep, pressures from home, odd dreams and the inevitable writer's block.

"Nothing to report," he said, when it was his turn.

Their focus for the day was the history of writing. Gill expounded at length and gave them a handout with a diagram purporting to show the arc of story. It was all too neat. In Morgan's experience, story was complicated by unreliable subjects, holes in timelines and editors who massacred your work with their red pens. Gill's theory, if accurate, could only exist in a theoretical world.

"Time to free-write," the man announced, lecture finished. "You have ten minutes to respond to the following prompt: What is story?"

Morgan opened his notebook but only to draw three-dimensional cubes and hairy dog faces. Next to him, Andrea was scrawling non-stop. He glanced over to see her opening line: 'Once upon a time is wired into our bones.'

Was that true? Was every experience already a story? Gill coughed and Morgan turned a page in his notebook; he wrote a few questions: *Are we born into story? Could our lives be anything other than story? Does any of this matter?*

"Now," Gill said, "I want you to think about your own story. Look at what you've written and apply those ideas to your own life. What are the main themes? Who are the central characters? You have twenty minutes to write and also take a comfort break. When we return, you will work together in pairs."

Bodies flocked to the door, and there was a jostle for the only bathroom that didn't require a walk to the main house. Morgan resisted the urge and made a word sketch of the room for his article: *octagonal space; endless windows; polished wood floor – walnut? A native drum propped against an inactive wood burner; BackJacks in a circle like upraised tombs.*

The tomb symbolism could be useful if Gill proved ruthless in murdering rough drafts. The man wasn't exactly critical, but he had a knack for conveying feedback through a question or even a neutral stare. Morgan glanced across at him; the upright posture and crisp suit conveyed mild disapproval. He put his notebook away and walked to the nearest window with his back towards Gill.

Across the meadow, a slender figure stood at the edge of a circle of stones. The woman, too far away for Morgan to identify, held a length of green material which she made dance with a flick of her wrists. The cloth rose and fell, surging wildly like emerald flame.

"Watching the wildlife?" Savannah asked, appearing at his shoulder. "Guess what? Gill has paired us up: Morgan and the Muse. Where shall we sit?"

"You choose," he said. "I need the restroom."

But when he tried the door of the shack, he found it locked and its occupant began to whistle a tune. Unable to wait any longer, Morgan slunk to the edge of the meadow and pissed into the long grass.

Reluctant to hurry back, he located the spot where he'd seen the woman with the scarf and found the crude outline of a labyrinth.

He recognized the design from a documentary he'd seen about Grace Cathedral. There were three stages to walking, as far as he could recall. The first had something to do with the shape of a life, but he couldn't remember the others. He was saved from this mental exertion by the sound of the gong, and he hurried back across the grass.

Savannah met him at the door with two large cushions under one arm. She led him to the far side of the room and offered him one of the cushions while she straddled the other as if riding a horse. Unwilling to mimic her action, Morgan slumped to the floor and cushioned his back against the glass. He tried to relax his body in the face of her commanding position.

The assignment was simple: each person had five minutes to describe their project and then the partner could ask questions. After that, they would switch roles.

"Your questions should help with content and form," Gill called out. "Make them count."

Around them, conversations sprouted like weeds and the room became thick with lost sons, disappointing spouses, heartaches of all kinds. But not a single character or story stepped forward from Morgan's life. He gestured for Savannah to go first but then regretted it as soon as she opened her mouth.

"You lost me after the portent of the foam on your latte," he quipped, ten minutes in to her speech.

"Where's your sense of mystery and wonder?"

"Strangled at birth. In my line of work, fantasy is not your friend."

"Tell me that doesn't look like a finger pointing to an island," Savannah insisted, holding out her phone.

"No finger, but I like the red coffee cup and the tiny macaroon."

She snatched the phone back and said it was his turn, but Morgan splayed his hands and looked vacant as Gill warned them time was nearly up.

"If you could write one story," Savannah urged, rocking back and forth on her cushion. "What story would you choose?"

"Maybe something about my dog, back when I was a kid," Morgan muttered, at last.

"What about your dog?"

"What he meant to me; what it was like when he was gone."

"There you are," she crowed, leaning forward to squeeze his shoulder and using it as a lever to stand up. "Dig into that story; that's where you'll find the magic. My work here is done. You can thank me later."

She sauntered off, all hips and attitude, but her blouse had caught in the waistband of her jeans and her legs appeared like a fragile stem for the over-inflated bust. Morgan smiled. Savannah was one crazy lady, but she had helped, pushing him like that. Maybe there was a story worth telling after all; he hadn't thought about his dog, Sideways, in years.

4

When the session resumed, Gill droned on about structure and pacing, but Morgan thought back to the day when a scruffy dog had landed in their kitchen. His father had been responsible for that – his one and only domestic victory. He'd found the dog abandoned by the side of the road and brought him home. Turning a deaf ear to his wife's hysterical warnings about disease, he hosed the dog down and plopped him into his son's willing lap.

"He's your responsibility now," his father had said. "We'll call him Sideways. He scuttled like a crab when he heard my truck."

Morgan had been eight-years-old, but he took the job seriously. He bought food from the local store with money from his father and saved dinner scraps when Margaret wasn't looking. He even went to the library for dog training tips, but Sideways was already familiar with basic commands which made his abandonment even worse.

"People re-locate," his father had explained. "They can't always take a dog with them."

"Or maybe he's lost and someone is out there looking," Margaret added. "Don't get too attached."

She had wanted to put a notice in the local paper and contact veterinarians within a thirty-mile radius of where the dog had been found, but John was implacable.

"There will be no such notice, Margaret," he said. "And no giving Sideways back to someone who could not take proper care of him in the first place."

Faith, late to the scene, had threatened a tantrum and Margaret was forced to relent. With some reluctance, she made room for a crate under her kitchen counter, the same spot she had hoped would house a dishwasher one day. The sacrifice made her bitter.

"Don't you go getting any ideas about taking him upstairs to your bedroom," she warned Morgan. "This is where he's going to sleep."

If he thought his mother would soften, that she would come to love Sideways in time, then Morgan was proved wrong. The dog sensed Margaret's disdain and behaved impeccably, respecting her rule over the kitchen with its olive-green surfaces, claw-foot fridge and deadly asbestos vinyl floor.

Weeks went by, and then months, but still Margaret treated Sideways like an undesired guest. Yet he was so much more: a comfort when physical storms lashed the house; a friend when Tom picked on his younger brother; an anchor when his mother disappeared behind closed doors. And on especially lonely nights, Morgan would make a nest in the crate under the kitchen counter and sleep with damp pajama pressed against rough hair.

If Margaret knew about these abominations, she turned a blind eye. She seemed to sense Sideways offered a physical comfort she herself had never been able to provide. She did her best to ignore the dog and resumed focus on the other significant blight in her world – a rust stain at the bottom of her kitchen sink.

Most mornings of Morgan's childhood, his mother worked the stain with slow circular movements that soon gave way to frenzied jabs. He would gaze past her bobbing head and count the jars of home-made jellies that stood to attention on her spotless shelves. When she failed to remove the stain, Margaret would cast around for other targets and it was then that Sideways came back into view.

"You spoil that dog," she accused Morgan. "He acts as if he's human."

And when her son spent fifty cents on a cushion at a garage sale, she snatched it away and asked why he had wasted his money on a dog. When he said it was because he loved Sideways, her mouth registered shock before it slid back into a grim smile as she handed the cushion back.

"Just keep his dirty paws off my clean floor," was all that she said.

Memories poured in and Morgan made copious hand-written notes. When they broke for lunch, he stayed behind and kept writing; when he finally emerged, he found Savannah waiting for him on the bench.

"I thought you were never going to stop," she exclaimed. "Was that the dog talking to you?"

"Maybe," he said. "Bits and pieces."

"You needed my inspiration," she affirmed, grabbing his arm and steering him up the path. "This world is full of wonders. Like those black specks on the bridge; do you know what they are?"

"Bark from the trees?" Morgan guessed, rubbing a few of them between his fingers.

"Wrong! Caterpillar shit. God's truth. The caterpillar munches the leaves and then poops them out. It is literally raining shit around here."

She cackled with laughter and skipped away as he tried to wipe his hand on her jeans, almost colliding with two women passing on the other side of the bridge.

"Viva la Muse!" one of the women muttered, under her breath.

"Bitch," Savannah muttered back, so softly only Morgan heard.

He studied their departing backs, and found there was something familiar in the way one of the women moved. When she half-turned, he recognized the green scarf from the meadow. As they followed behind, he strained to hear the women's conversation, but only laugher drifted back to him like teasing clouds.

Captive at the lunch table, Morgan spooned lasagna into his mouth and smiled when necessary. Savannah was holding court, and the woman from the meadow was out of reach at the far end of the table.

The press of female bodies and the high-pitched chatter reminded him of days in his mother's kitchen with Faith's adolescent friends. From a safe place under the table, he would watch the jiggle of their pale knees and the tap of Mary Janes on the vinyl floor. Sweet, stolen moments in a forest of talcum powder legs, until, inevitably, his mother would spy him and haul him out.

"You shouldn't be here," she would say. "Girls only. Go outside and play."

He would trudge to the door, take a last look at the happy faces and witness his mother nodding approval to everyone but him.

"What do you think?" Savannah nudged his side.

"About what?"

"About dreams and whether it's possible to write them into a text. Can it work?"

"I don't remember my dreams," Morgan confessed.

Savannah rolled her eyes and turned back to her conversation as Morgan reached for the salad. If you could call such a complex mix of greens, fetta, pumpkin seeds and pomegranate a salad. Kim might. On weekends, she had experimented with new dishes, and the kitchen would be littered with spice jars, tasting spoons and dishes piled high in their narrow sink. He had loved the contrast with Margaret's antiseptic style.

"Dreams show us what we are afraid to experience in real life," said a voice, from the far end of the table.

Heads turned, but the speaker faced away from them as she rinsed her plate and loaded it into the dishwasher.

"What do you mean, Eve?" Savannah demanded.

She got no response. Eve took a mug from the corner cupboard and walked slowly out of the room.

"Well!" Savannah spat out the word. "According to that theory, I want to get up close with a bat, grow wings and declare myself queen of the animal kingdom."

"I don't think she meant it literally," Morgan said, amid the laughter.

"What do you know?" Savannah snapped. "You don't even remember your dreams."

Morgan finished his salad, left the table and nested his plate in the dishwasher next to the one left by Eve. Now that he knew her name, he drew out the single syllable in his head like a chant that could conjure her into being.

But there was no sign of her out in the courtyard, and the building opposite gave nothing away. He was still peering at one of the windows when Savannah exited the kitchen and gave him a quizzical look. She had her hands on her hips, as if about to call out a wayward husband. But instead of a reprimand, she asked if he wanted to come into town for coffee and cake.

"Some other day," he said. "I want to keep writing while things feel fresh."

"Suit yourself," she shrugged.

It was quiet in the courtyard after she left. Even the hummingbirds had deserted the half-empty feeders. Morgan had read somewhere that a hummingbird beats its wings seventy times a second in normal flight and two hundred times during a high-speed dive. It was impossible to imagine – those poor, frantic beating hearts.

He chose a table, angled his chair towards Eve's building and opened his notebook. He chose a fresh page, wrote *Sideways* at the top and then began to describe his dog: *His hair was rough like a boot brush, but his ears were soft like paper.*

He snuffled to show pleasure and loved bacon smuggled under the table. Sideways showed up and made us all better.

The more he wrote, the easier it was to tune his senses back to those days with the tang of bleach, the rustle of his mother's starched apron, the feel of a cold wet nose pressed against his leg. One day in particular stood out. It was two weeks after the dog had arrived, and Morgan had sought out his father who was reading a newspaper out on the porch. He'd cleared his throat, and John had lowered the newspaper and ordered him to spit it out.

"It would be nice to walk Sideways together some time," he'd blurted, hopping from one foot to the other.

His father had smiled slightly and then resumed reading until Sideways began to bark and the newspaper lowered once more.

"Go play with him, son," his father said. "I'm busy. Go play with him; that's what he's for."

Morgan had trailed away, hoping that his father would call him back. But the call never came. That was when he knew. It was blindingly obvious. Sideways was the only one who would never let him down.

Morgan wrote in a daze, his fingers cramped from the effort it took to keep pace with his memory. He wrote until he felt wrung dry, and only then did his thoughts go back to Eve. He returned the notebook to his canvas bag and edged closer to her building.

Aware of his absurdity, he pressed his nose against the window like a thief. On the inside window-ledge, he saw three empty beer bottles; a fourth had been pressed into service as a vase. Beyond them, a coffee press commanded a wooden table along with a five-high pile of books. He squinted, but he could not make out any of the titles.

At some point, Eve would return to fill the coffee press or arrange fresh flowers in the makeshift vase. A feeling like grief passed though him. Those signature acts of intimacy would happen without his knowledge.

5

Morgan walked and then ran towards the meadow, ignoring the damp grass that stained his boots and soaked his socks. At the opening to the labyrinth, he bent double and caught his breath. He pictured the bodies in Grace Cathedral, drifting like ghosts in a perfectly proportioned wheel, and his body began to calm.

When he entered the circle, he closed his eyes and a kind of hypnotism took hold. His mind drifted back into the past, but when he stubbed his right big toe on a rock, his eyes flew open. He swore loudly and a rabbit startled into the long grass.

He had tasted rabbit twice in his life. Once with Kim at a fancy restaurant and years earlier when Tom 'accidentally' shot Faith's pet rabbit with a pellet gun. Morgan had never seen his father so angry; he told his son it was 'beyond careless' and got even angrier when Tom mumbled that it was 'just a rabbit.'

"Just a rabbit? I'll show you just a rabbit," he had stormed.

He insisted Tom finish the creature off, showed him how to execute the neck twist, and made him harvest the kill. Tom cried through the whole ordeal while Faith became hysterical. She had wanted to bury the rabbit and hold a ceremony, but this was rural Wisconsin and the creature was destined for the pot.

"There will be no waste," his father intoned, during the somber dinner.

The meat was tough, and Morgan left a ring of half-chewed pieces on the edge of his plate. Faith escaped to her room and refused to come out. Only Tom finished a full serving and won back their father's approval.

That night, both brothers woke with sore bellies and Margaret had to make them stomach-settling tea. She explained that John hated cruelty towards animals and that his own father had been a hard man. Then she read to them from the Bible, her voice low and filled with gravel as she played the part of Samson in the story of the man whose power resided in his hair.

Morgan had been transfixed. He hadn't followed the tenuous link made between the rabbit and a woman called Delilah, but he loved the idea of magical hair. Only later, tugging on Tom's pajama sleeve, did he ask in a whisper: "What is seduced?"

By morning, the culprit had been forgiven, not least because he'd pledged to buy his sister a new and better rabbit. Morgan, meanwhile, remained obsessed with Samson's hair. He begged his mother to let him grow his own hair long, pestered her for weeks, and finally wore her down. He missed one, two, three visits to the barber. Each week, he measured his hair with a ruler and kept a record of its growth.

In the relatively short time that his hair grew long, Morgan gained proof of its power. His mother became unexpectedly tender. She would snatch up a brush, pull it more or less gently through his locks, and call him her Celtic Prince. She explained that his name had origins in Ireland, Scotland and Wales, and one of its meanings was 'Defender of the Sea.'

"But we don't live near an ocean," he'd objected, "so it doesn't count."

"We don't," Margaret agreed, "but you can live far from water and still be afraid of drowning."

At the center of the labyrinth, Morgan lay on the ground and curled himself into a ball. Back then, he hadn't understood his mother's words, but now he felt they were proof of a vulnerability she almost never expressed.

His special status hadn't lasted long. How could it? On the first day back at school after a break, kids with nothing to lose grabbed him at recess and pinned him down. Amidst whoops and hollers, they hacked off chunks of his hair with a blunt and rusty pocket-knife. When a teacher appeared and the bullies evaporated, Morgan was left fighting back tears. As he waited for his mother to come, he gathered up chunks of mutilated hair.

"We committed the sin of pride," Margaret said, during the long ride back to the farm. "Nothing good comes of drawing attention to yourself; nothing good."

In the kitchen, she made him release fistfuls of hair and cut off the last of his curls. She cast all of it into the embers of the living room fire, and, for days, the house smelled like burned rubber.

Margaret was cold; Tom was indifferent; even Faith lost interest in the story after a few days, while his father acted as if nothing had happened. Only Sideways understood. On the day of the hair disaster, he crept upstairs, pushed his nose under the protective huddle of Morgan's arms and licked away his tears.

He'd felt so utterly rejected, but now, from a different perspective, Morgan glimpsed a whole new dimension to his mother's response. She was not merely the all-powerful punishing figure, but a woman afraid for her son. She had wanted, and failed, to keep him safe.

The labyrinth had done its work; the past was not as fixed as Morgan had imagined but a living, malleable story.

He got to his feet and staggered back to his cabin where he slept deeply for the first time in months.

Refreshed, he arrived at the evening session ready to write, but Gill detonated any such delusions. There was something uncanny about the man's ability to sense the room. He put them back into pairs and asked them to recall a photograph that captured a significant moment in their early lives. Then, he told them to add the people, events and feelings that were outside the frame.

Morgan was paired with Robin this time, and she volunteered to go first. She described a photograph of herself as a toddler covered head-to-toe in chalk; she had just decorated the neighbors' driveway. Out of frame, her embarrassed father apologized, while her mother took the photograph of the scene. Robin had drawn a row of purple flowers and two pumpkins doing a dance.

"That was the day I discovered my passion for art," she told him. "But it has taken this long to get back there. I never gave myself permission. Goodness, I sound like a Hallmark movie. Your turn."

Morgan felt the usual blank. Had his parents even owned a camera? He had no memory of holiday snaps, just the one family portrait over the fireplace commissioned when Tom graduated from high school. He was about to tell Robin she might as well go again, when he felt her warm hand on his knee.

"Close your eyes for a moment," she coaxed, "and imagine yourself as a child. You're at home, walking between different rooms. Maybe there's a framed photograph or a family album. Take a good look around."

Morgan quelled his rising panic and tried to follow her instructions. But there were no family albums or framed photographs, nothing until he entered his parents' bedroom at the end of the tour. All of a sudden, he saw himself holding a black-and-white photograph of his mother with a new-born baby in her arms.

"I'm in my parents' bedroom," he said aloud, eyes still closed. "I'm not supposed to be here. Everyone is at Tom's graduation. No, that's not right. Faith is home, but she's in her room with the door shut. I'm bored, and that's why I'm in my parents' bedroom."

He cracked his eyes open. Robin had tilted her head in the way of a professional listener; he shut them again and kept going. He described the room with its closed curtains, tight-lipped bed and antique dresser; it was the dresser that had fascinated him that day, as if he knew it held secrets.

He'd started at the bottom, his father's domain, and found socks, underpants and sweaters. It bothered him that a tall man would have to bend low simply to get dressed in the morning. The middle drawer held sleepwear that belonged to them both. That left the top drawer, home to his mother's most private garments. It was there, hidden among stockings and slips, that he found the heavily-creased photograph.

In the snapshot, his mother had sunken cheeks and heavy eyes; she was standing outside what looked like a hospital. His father must have taken the shot, proving the existence of a camera, and he had focused the lens on the bundle clutched in his wife's arms.

"What struck you about the photograph?" Robin asked. "What stays with you now?"

How could he describe what he saw? His mother, her hand raised over the new-born, had a wild expression that could have been love or some darker emotion. Was she about to caress her child or smother its cries?

Robin's hand left his knee, but only so she could wrap her arms around him and draw his head down to her chest. He was astonished to find he was crying. He told her, in a muffled voice, that he put the photograph back in the drawer. Precious memory or shameful memento, it was no business of his.

Gill announced the end of the exercise, and Morgan

slipped out of Robin's hold, trying to appear as if he was stretching. No one seemed to have noticed his distress, so he returned to his seat and scribbled notes as Gill talked about the power of repressed memory. It wasn't until later, back in his cabin, that he allowed himself full expression. After the torrent, he lay with his eyes closed so tight he could see his own stars.

In the morning, the air was thick with moisture and his porthole window had fogged. He rubbed it clear with an elbow and peered out at sodden branches and a litter of leaves on the ground. The storm had passed. It was early, but he walked barefoot up the path in his boxers to the outdoor shower.

Wood chips stuck to his feet, and he thought of Kim and her beauty rituals. He used to make fun of her mud-caked face and the plugs that separated her toes. When she was plucked, steamed and exfoliated, he would run his hand from ankle to thigh and whistle his praises. In truth, he preferred her legs rough and the tang of sweat to any of her lotions and perfumes. He had just never told her that.

The shower was a narrow pipe that hung over a soap-scummed pallet. When the water ran warm, he slipped off his boxers and scrubbed his body with a sliver of soap. A quick rinse, and then he wrapped his towel around his waist and jogged back to the cabin. He chose fresh underwear, stiff jeans, a check-shirt and the previous days' mismatched socks and walked up to the kitchen.

The place was empty, and Morgan was relieved he'd avoided the intimacy of breakfast and the prospect of Robin's pity or compassion. He made coffee and buttered two slices of bread which he carried down to the gathering space well ahead of the women. Once he'd eaten, he worked on the draft of an article for Zoe; by the time the room filled, he was approaching solid ground.

But then the ground shifted; the anticipated forty-eight

hours of silence had turned the women skittish. Fifteen minutes into the session, Gill cut the chatter by sounding the metal bowl.

"Enough," he said, voice raised. "You're all over the place. We need a positive distraction. I don't typically do this, but today is a special day for one of us. Morgan, do you mind if we make a fuss of you?"

All eyes turned to him, and he wondered if Robin had breached his confidence and revealed the breakdown. But when he looked at her across the circle, she offered a reassuring smile.

"Can we sing Happy Birthday?" Gill asked, "Or is it too much of a cliché?"

"Sing!" the women cried, in response.

Christ. He had actually forgotten his own birthday. Kim must have flagged the date when she sent in his application. He opened his mouth to protest, but Savannah had already started singing. The others joined in with her slightly staged vibrato, and they ended with a series of whoops and cries.

"Have you discovered the secret of the hole?" Gill asked, when it was quiet again.

"The hole?"

He pointed to the rock which lay in the bowl next to Robin's painting. Savannah's laminated card had been set to one side.

"I suppose I have," Morgan said, reluctantly. "I've discovered stories where I thought there was a gap."

"Good," Gill said, his voice warm. "Now you are ready to write. Don't let anything else distract you."

6

The morning moved on with Gill addressing character and tension, but Morgan could no longer hear or process his words. A series of birthdays had flashed into memory – fruit cakes his mother made when she knew he preferred chocolate sponge; also presents that included books on personal hygiene and a junior razor given long before he needed to shave. And then there was the year everyone forgot because Tom did something heroic on the baseball team.

As the morning expired, Morgan felt himself become porous, as if the exercise with Robin had removed safeguards and the sensory impressions of childhood could invade his body. He smelled the burnt hay of his father's pipe; the stench of Margaret's Magnolia perfume; the musk of mothballs hidden under stockings in the forbidden drawer. There were sounds too - arguments behind closed doors and silences when his father retreated to the shed or his mother escaped to her sewing.

"Now is the time to raise concerns," Gill was saying. "You have two full days of writing ahead with no distraction. That might excite you or fill you with dread. Be honest – if one of you has a fear or concern, it could help the others. Yes, Eve?"

"It's probably not what you're after," she said, "but Jess and I hit a roadblock last night. So, we played that game where you choose who you would sleep with, marry or avoid."

She paused and delivered her killer line: "We both agreed we would sleep with Morgan. Not because he's the only man, we find his auburn locks deeply moving."

Laughter ruptured the room and inserted itself under thin skin like a layer of contaminate. Morgan smoothed his hair with unconscious fingers, wrote a few lines in his notebook, and looked up to find Gill was the only one not laughing. No, not the only one, Savannah looked more disgusted than amused.

"Now that's out of everyone's system," Gill admonished them, "let's break for lunch."

Feet shuffled to the exit, but Morgan remained bent over his notebook until a shadow fell on the page.

"Someone was the center of attention," Savannah teased, ruffling his hair.

"I'm an easy target," he said, glumly. "But I don't think she meant anything by it, really, she was just messing around."

"Not Eve. She's transparent. I meant Gill. Don't you think he was a little too interested in your hole?"

"Do you have to be so crude?"

"I call them like I see them, honey. Don't kill the messenger just because I'm alive from the neck down. So, how shall we celebrate your birthday?"

"I think we already did."

"I mean for real. It's our last chance to hit town before we're thrown into silence."

Morgan studied her face; for the first time, he noticed dark circles under her eyes that were visible despite the make-up. For all her seeming confidence, things were not entirely peachy with Savannah.

"What about lunch here?" he asked.

"Seriously? We can get something in town."

"Okay. Okay. But you're buying."

"Deal. Meet me out front in ten."

Morgan took his time; he shuffled around the cabin and then made his bed for the first time. He couldn't quite shake the effect of Eve's words. Gill had made light of it, but Morgan felt caught in those sly syllables; like a sticky sensual fly paper, they had left a residue of longing.

The 'quaint little island town' advertised in guidebooks, was crawling with tourists when they arrived. Women, not rocking the nautical look, lumbered in and out of stores, while their kids, limp-faced with boredom, endured the madness for the price of sugary drinks.

"Stick with me," Savannah ordered. "I know where there's great coffee and killer fish and fries. Ignore the tourist trash."

Trash it was: candles pressed with fake flowers, seascapes adrift in driftwood frames, buckets and spades shipped all the way from China. Down a side alley, Morgan glimpsed the harbor where a restaurant loomed over the water like an ungainly bird. Ten minutes later, they were tucked into one of the booths, and he had lost Savannah's attention which drifted continually to the bar.

"The place is run by a Scottish dude," she told him. "I can't understand a word he says, but he knows his fish and fries."

"Chips," said Morgan. "They call them chips."

"Whatever they're called, we have to have some. I'll order for us both."

She sauntered to the bar and hailed a bearded man Morgan assumed was the owner. He heard her laugh and watched her write something on a napkin before pressing it to her lips. Bearded man received the napkin with both hands and brought it to his heart.

"What was all that about?" Morgan asked, when Savannah returned with two beers.

"He's convinced I'm somebody; I was forced to tell him I'm on the stage."

When bearded man brought their fish and chips in person, he begged Morgan to take a photograph of him with Savannah. She put her arm around him and pretended to lick his face.

"I've lost my appetite," Morgan complained, when they were alone again.

"Lighten up; it's all in fun. He's married, and I have someone at home."

She showed him a photograph of a wiry man hunched over an electric guitar. He was half her size in all obvious dimensions, as Morgan couldn't help observing.

"Oh no, honey. Trust me," Savannah replied. "He's anything but small."

Morgan choked on his beer, and Savannah had to pound his back, laughing at his discomfort.

"It's as if you've lived in a monastery," she teased. "When Eve made that comment in the circle, you turned so red I nearly pulled the fire alarm."

"She caught me off guard."

"She scared the hell out of you, admit it."

Morgan took refuge in his food, but the fish was salty and the chips doused in vinegar. The sexual banter felt exhausting. Savannah had moved on from her own exploits to consider Gill's, picturing him with a much younger man. He escaped, briefly, to the restroom, but when he returned, bearded man had taken his seat; he was still trying to pin down Savannah's supposed celebrity.

"You enjoy playing with people, don't you?" Morgan said, when they were out on the street.

"Nobody died," Savannah said. "I will, though, if I don't get something for my headache."

While Savannah checked out a pharmacy, Morgan went into a gift shop filled with sarongs. He bought a journal with an elephant on the cover, and told Savannah it was to keep his personal writing separate from his work. She told him that it would do him good to get a little messy.

They didn't speak on the drive back. Savannah seemed to have forgotten it was his birthday, and she made no mention of it when they parted ways. He told himself it didn't matter.

When the circle gathered again in the late afternoon, the morning's giddiness had given way to static tension. The room held a charge the way sky holds electricity before a storm. Gill acknowledged their mood and offered tips to get through the next forty-eight hours.

"If you have a legitimate need," he said, "you can signal me to step away from the property. But only if it's absolutely necessary. I want this silence to be a strong and effective container. If there's nothing else, let's begin."

One-by-one, they filed out of the room, faces masked in concentration, as if silence was a high-wire act. Morgan felt unable to leave his seat. He studied Gill's handout on the art and practice of solitude. It was written in tight little paragraphs, dense prose that was almost a labyrinth of writing. How many hours, days, weeks had it taken the writer to find this exact combination of words? It took guts and muscle to write.

He closed his eyes and pictured various spots on the property where he could write: his cabin; the bench under the pine tree; the porch near the hummingbird feeders; the back deck with its view over the marsh. He shivered with potent energy. At that precise moment, he felt pressure against his cheek and inhaled the scent of lavender.

"Happy birthday," said a voice in his ear. "I love the mismatched socks."

Two small objects were pressed firmly into the palm of his left hand, and he curled his fingers reflexively. He stayed that way for several long moments, and when he opened his eyes, Eve had gone. His released his held breath and unclenched his hand.

When he looked down, he found a silver coin embossed with a sitting Buddha, and, next to it, a child's simple wooden spinning top.

7

Out in the vestibule, Morgan paused by a suede pouch that hung from a hook on the wall. All week, women had pulled runes from the pouch and talked about their significance. He had thought it foolish. But now, fresh from his encounter with Eve, Morgan dipped his hand in and pulled out a smooth white stone. The first side was blank. He turned it over, but the other side was the same. He tossed it back into the pouch. A waste of time, just as he had thought.

Back in his cabin, he lay the Buddha emblem flat on his desk and balanced the spinning top in one of many grooves. With both objects in his peripheral vision, he sought a way back into his story. But as he toyed with words, read sentences aloud, removed paragraphs and returned them, Eve's presence would intrude. He'd imagine her knelt beside him, recall the precise inflection of her words, feel the pressure on his cheek.

Frustrated, he picked up the spinning top and whirled it in the palm of his hand, but it leaped away from him like a demon and disappeared under the bed. On all fours, he searched for the object among the tumbleweeds of dust.

It was then, down on all fours, that he thought about the final time Sideways had made it upstairs to his room. The dog's decline had been gradual: he no longer greeted Morgan at the door; he stopped following him from room-to-room; eventually, he spent most of his day asleep. Morgan, preoccupied with school and happy to have made friends at last, failed to grasp the significance of the slowdown.

Late one night, he heard the snuff of a muzzle against the bottom of his bedroom door. It was Sideways, panting with exertion, and Morgan had lifted the dog onto his bed. For a while, he rubbed Sideways' ears and ran fingers along his belly. When the dog began to snore, Morgan tucked him in under the covers.

The pair slept late, and Margaret had to rouse them in the morning. When she wrenched back the covers, she shrieked at the sight of the dog and her husband came running. She shooed Morgan into the bathroom, and he remembered thinking that his friend had been remarkably still.

As Morgan recovered the dusty spinning top, he sat back on his haunches. He could see his mother, prim in her dressing gown, recoiled from the intimacy of the bedroom scene. His father had arrived and been stern; he ordered Morgan to get dressed, make his own breakfast and take the bus to school. As Morgan left the bedroom, the only sign that Sideways had been there was a slight dent in the mattress and the faintest hint of warmth.

He never saw his friend again. For one whole week, he had wondered if he had killed Sideways by rolling on him in his sleep. It was Tom, back from summer camp, who told him a better story. Sideways had died of old age; it was no one's fault. Their father had taken the body and buried him in the woods; it was his version of being kind.

Together, the brothers searched the woods until they found freshly disturbed earth. As they stared down at the mound, Tom suggested they make a marker. They gathered twigs, shaped them into a dog bone, and bound them with bits of string Tom had in his pocket. When they placed the marker, Morgan trembled like an aspen until Tom flung an arm over his shoulder.

"Looks like he went deep to make it safe from coyotes," Tom said. "That was nice. You know how he hates it when any of us are sad."

But the thought of coyotes only made Morgan cry harder. He was crying now, as other memories silted up from his unconscious, as if they sensed their moment had come. The day he crashed his kite and his father had called him reckless; the promised camping adventure that never came; Tom's graffiti on his 'Improved Writer' award; those tortuous shopping trips with his mother that softened when his hair grew but hardened again soon after.

Morgan clutched the spinning top and rocked back and forth while weird sounds emerged from his belly. He skipped breakfast, crawled onto his bed and slept. He dreamed that Eve was in league with Tom and Savannah was fighting his mother. He lurched awake in a tangle of acrimony and tears.

By midday, the needs of his stomach forced him to wash his face and leave the cabin. He'd written nothing since the enforced silence. In the courtyard, he walked past Eve's downstairs window and noticed the flowers had wilted and there were three new beer bottles on the ledge.

Lunch was laid out buffet style, so he heaped his plate and ate alone at one of the courtyard tables. He stayed there most of the afternoon, typing up inadequate paragraphs for Zoe. He took pot shots at vegetarians and made fun of his efforts to sit cross-legged and his attempts to find his voice in a group of middle-aged women.

In the late lazy afternoon, Savannah rolled into the courtyard with her laptop and wads of toilet paper. She sat three tables away and dabbed at her keyboard for a while.

When she felt his gaze, she pantomimed a walk with two fingers and he gave a thumbs up. They had barely hit the tarmac when she let fly.

"I am so over this fucking silence. Someone just 'shushed' me when I took my laptop inside. All I said was I'd be back. I was this close to ripping her a new one."

"Can I quote you on that?"

"You can quote me all over town; writers with their panties in a wad are the worst."

"Zoe's going to love you. Are you getting any actual writing done?"

"I was, until I spilled wine on my keyboard. I've spent the last few hours drying it out."

"You're a journalist's dream," Morgan laughed.

"Then come with me tomorrow when I go meet Gill at his house. You could be my witness."

"Why are you going to his house? How the hell did you wrangle that?"

"Persistence, baby. I don't take no for an answer. I want him to hear my story and tell me I'm on track. Come on, you know you want to be there."

Even as he played for time, Morgan knew that she was right. He would be the passive point in their triangle, but he'd endured worse for a story. Gill's home would hold vital clues to his character. He might be a collector or a hoarder whose public and private image were at odds. As Savannah prattled on, Morgan ran scenarios in his head.

When the light began to fade, they turned back and grew quiet as they approached the courtyard. Savannah put her finger to her lips and tiptoed in an exaggerated manner. But instead of silence, they heard laugher from somewhere above their heads.

"I guess we're not the only rebels," she said.

"Shall we see who it is?" Morgan asked.

But Savannah wanted to go back to her room. She had half-decent whisky or cheap wine, and he was welcome to either or both.

"I want to see who's up there," Morgan persisted.

"You know who's up there," Savannah said, but she followed as Morgan opened the door to Eve's building and climbed the first set of stairs.

"Come in," a voice said, when he knocked. "No naked ladies; you're safe to enter here."

Without stopping to wonder at Eve's choice of words, Morgan flung the door wide. His first impression was a room full of beds - four singles in a space made for two. They were pushed together, but each had a singular role: two were for sleeping, one was an impromptu bar, and the fourth was covered with papers and books. Eve sat at one end of a bed, propped up by pillows, and Jess sat opposite with a manuscript on her lap.

"What's so funny?" Morgan asked, as Savannah stirred restlessly at his side.

"Your faces," Eve gasped. "You look as if you've stumbled on an orgy."

"Y'all, this feels like a private party," Savannah said, pulling on Morgan's arm.

"Not unless you make it that way," Eve countered. "Pull up a chair. Jess is just reading her latest draft."

There were no chairs in sight, so Morgan perched on a bed while Savannah remained standing.

"I'll start again," Jess said. "There really is a chair in the bathroom; just throw my nightdress out of the way. And get yourselves a beer before Eve drinks the last one."

Morgan retrieved the chair for Savannah. He hadn't felt right about moving the nightgown, so he'd left it draped on the back of the chair. Savannah threw it onto a bed and reached for a beer which she opened with her fist, using the edge of a night table. She drank then handed the bottle to Morgan.

"You can have this," she said. "I won't be here long, but it looks like you might."

"Let's just hear Jess read," he begged.

"*The Weight of a Father*," Jess intoned. "That's the title. Not sure if it's any good."

Her story began on the day they took her father's emaciated body to the morgue and worked back through long months of his illness. She tracked his refusal to eat, his nightmares, his rides into mania and dips back down into depression. By the time she ended, she was back at the funeral scene with her fingers crushed in her mother's trembling hand. Morgan was hunched over. It was Eve who broke the silence and toasted the girl who had survived all that; she called the language piercing.

"What else?" asked Jess. "Did the first-person work? Would you change anything?"

Savannah cleared her throat, and Morgan interjected before she could say anything crass.

"It's not easy to comment on something as intimate and powerful as that," he said.

"Do it anyway," Jess insisted.

"You made me question reality," he admitted. "Who is to say that your father's world was any less real than yours or mine? And that detail of ninety-eight pounds; that detail slayed me."

Jess nodded, and Eve smiled her approval while Savannah got to her feet.

"You guys," she said, "I'm heading out. Thanks for that, Jess. It was... I don't have the words."

Morgan half-rose, as if to accompany her, then sat back down. He listened to the muffled tread of her feet as she went down the stairs.

"The muse has lost all power of speech," Eve laughed. "Struck dumb by your brilliance, Jess. Either that or she disapproves. I think she might be a little jealous."

"Jealous?" Morgan echoed.

"Jealous," Eve confirmed. "But let's forget about her. What about you? Aren't you afraid to be alone with such dangerous women?"

Morgan laughed, although he did feel more exposed now Savannah had gone. He muttered about it getting late.

"No need to rush off," Eve said. "We don't bite. It's my turn to read. I'll take it personally if you go now."

"You can have my spot," Jess offered. "I'll listen from a horizontal position, if that's okay, Eve?"

Morgan replaced Jess on the bed, but angled himself against the wall and left a generous space between himself and Eve.

"I'm glad you're here," she said, smiling slightly. "I have something to give you."

"You've already given me gifts. Thank you for those by the way. I wasn't sure of their significance."

"No significance. Just a gift. Like this one," she said, slipping a piece of card into his bag. "You can look at it later."

She lifted her papers and began to read. Her voice, soft as smoke, drifted languidly into Morgan's brain; he felt himself part of her story and of the whole intimate scene.

8

"Where did *you* sleep last night?" Savannah asked, blocking Morgan's path. "Don't act all innocent. What happened last night after I left?"

"Nothing happened."

"I left you alone in a bedroom with two women, one of whom has a major crush on you, and nothing happened?"

"I just listened to them read. Nothing happened," he repeated, sidestepping Savannah for the coffee.

"So why did Lily see you creep through the courtyard at six this morning?"

"She didn't."

"No, but she did see you walk pass the shower, and you scared the crap out of her. And I can see that you're still wearing yesterday's clothes."

"What are you, the retreat police? I fell asleep in their room. End of story."

"Sounds more like a beginning to me. Men are such suckers."

"Then why did you leave me there?" he asked. "Anyway, we're supposed to be in silence."

"You didn't mind breaking silence last night," she pointed out. "I'll see you in an hour for our meeting with

46

Gill; don't be late."

By the time they met up in the parking lot, Morgan was sure the whole thing was a bad idea. Gill was a busy man, and the point of silence was figuring things out on their own. Savannah told him not to be a pussy.

"It's a good opportunity for us both," she said.

"From a professional standpoint," he replied.

"Then get your professional ass into my car."

They drove in silence. Savannah was either focused on the road or psyching herself up to meet Gill. Grateful for this respite, Morgan replayed in his mind what had been an unexpected night. When Eve had told him she was married, he'd assumed the boundary was clear. As a result, his sleep next to her had been untroubled by either longing or fantasy.

When he woke, Eve was propped up on her pillows in much the same position as the night before. For a moment, he wondered if she'd been awake all night, but then he recalled the surrender of her narrow waist, the knobs of bone along her spine, the whispered plea to 'hold me, just hold me'. He had cradled her for much of the night.

He recalled that she had seemed annoyed at how well he had slept. Apparently, her night had been restless; she had barely slept a wink. He asked if he'd disturbed her.

"Not in the way you think," she told him. "Let's just say that having you close was a little...agitating. I felt like a teenager with a crush."

He'd apologized, although he hadn't done anything wrong, and Eve replied that the body wanted what the body wanted. When she threw him out of her room, he walked back to the cabin wondering exactly what it was her body *had* wanted; it seemed presumptuous to hope.

"Can you read those house numbers?" Savannah asked, interrupting his thoughts.

She had turned down onto a side road and was driving slowly as she looked left to right at the various houses.

47

There were single story units with yards that were littered with toys, a tasteful two-storey tucked among trees, and a duplex with an oversized garage.

"I bet that's the one we're after," Morgan replied, pointing to a modern glass box.

But Gill's house turned out to be a modest ranch further down the lane. They could see his silhouette through the picture window; he was talking on the phone. Savannah parked and then checked her makeup in the rear-view mirror. She bared her teeth and rubbed at a lipstick smear with her little finger.

They were halfway up the steps to the front door when it was flung open; Gill ushered them into his living room, mouthing an apology as he was still on his call.

"Sorry," he said, when he returned five minutes later. "Agents, boyfriends and publishers are all quite demanding."

Afraid that Savannah might ask which category had been on the phone, Morgan said something nice about the house and setting. Gill nodded, as if used to such praise, and offered them coffee. Morgan followed him out to the kitchen, appraising the layout of the house as he went. Gill was clearly an avid reader, no surprise there, and had a penchant for black-and-white photography. The house was spotless but not cold.

"You're probably wondering why I'm here," he ventured, as Gill turned on the kettle.

"Don't worry. I can read between the lines."

They shared a smile, and when the coffee was ready, Morgan carried the tray out to Savannah.

"Is that where you write?" he asked Gill, pointing to a mahogany desk staged with paper and pens.

"Off the record?" Gill checked. "The truth is, I usually write in bed, but journalists like the idea of a dedicated desk; I don't like to disabuse them."

"I'm not here as a journalist," Morgan smiled.

"I know. That's why I told the truth."

Before he could ask a follow-up question, Savannah claimed the stage. She thanked them for coming, as if they were her guests, and began to spew her story. She used Morgan's name, as if he had directly authorized the re-telling. He moved away from her and stood near the picture window.

It was a clear day, and he watched a tanker heave its rusted bulk through Puget Sound. Heavy with freight, the vessel seemed incongruous against the backdrop of snow-capped mountain. Morgan had felt something similar waking up next to Eve - out of place and clumsy in her presence. She'd offered him coffee, but in a half-hearted way, and then he'd thanked her for a memorable night.

"I'm glad one of us got what we needed," Eve had sighed.

He hadn't lingered. When he passed the outdoor shower, someone had pulled the curtain tight with a snap. He knew now that this was Lily. He had quickened his pace, made it to the bridge, and unzipped his fly to send a shimmering stream into the marsh. As the drops scattered over the leaves of the skunk cabbage, he'd felt glad he hadn't sullied Eve's personal space.

As if the memory created an urge, he asked Gill for directions to the restroom. Once there, he ignored the hand-written sign about saving water and pulled the flush. Then, he checked for spillage and wiped the seat before washing his hands and leaving the countertop dry.

When he got back, Gill was in the kitchen loading their mugs into the dishwasher. He asked Morgan, in an undertone, what it was that Savannah wanted.

"Inspiration? Insight? An agent? Honestly, I have no idea," Morgan confessed.

"If Colin was here, he would ask her point blank," Gill said, and pointed to a photograph on the wall behind Morgan's head. "That shot was taken in the state park just down the road. The tree he's leaning against is more than

49

five-hundred-years old. My Colin was a champion of the environment long before it became fashionable."

Morgan studied the photograph, aware now that Colin was the subject of most of the prints on the walls. He had questions, but Gill's face had closed its shutters.

"You two look chummy," Savannah commented, when they returned to her. "Anything I should know?"

Plenty, thought Morgan, but he kept that to himself. Before she could pick up steam again, he asked if Gill was working on anything new.

"Writers don't talk about works-in-progress," Gill admonished. "You know that."

Morgan nodded but tilted his head and smiled.

"Okay. Okay," Gill laughed. "A few non-fiction essays, sketches really, about someone who meant a great deal to me. And that's all you're getting."

"We know how busy you must be," Morgan replied, taking the hint. "We should get back to the retreat and at least look as if we've been preserving silence."

Gill laughed again and said something about the teacher corrupting his students. He walked with them to the door; he would have shaken Savannah's hand, only she pulled him into an embrace.

"Do you write book blurbs?" she asked, as she released him. "Or recommend writers to your agent?"

"Never," Gill replied. "I don't get involved. A book rises and falls on its own merits. From what I heard today, Savannah, you know exactly what you are doing."

She flounced away from him and Morgan would have followed, but Gill gripped his arm and pulled him close. He spoke softly, close to Morgan's ear, in a cloud of musky cologne and coffee-infused breath.

"Don't give up on your writing," Gill urged. "Your story is not as dramatic, but it's of equal value."

The pressure on his arm released, and Morgan stumbled down the steps after Savannah. The car was idling, and they were back on the highway within minutes.

"What a bust," Savannah declared. "I think you had more to say about my story than he did. I'm not sure he even bothered to listen."

"He listened. Didn't you hear him say that you were on track? That's high praise from an author."

"But what did I really gain? Nothing tangible."

"So, you were after an agent?"

"Would it have killed him? And you suck as a wingman, by the way."

"You're a piece of work," Morgan sighed.

Official silence was over at dinner, but Morgan barely spoke as he shoveled vegetarian chili. Eve was absent, so there was no incentive to linger; he was still mulling the intensity with which Gill had delivered his final words.

Down at the gathering space, he waited impatiently for the first reading session to begin. When the women arrived, their energy felt expectant, as if the silence had produced a chemical change. Eve was the last to arrive, and Morgan studied his bed-mate of the night before. She had on a pair of white overalls with a sprig of wilted green in the breast pocket and seemed unusually pale. He wondered if she was sad that the retreat was almost over. As if she knew he was thinking of her, she glanced across the circle and her smile carried a faint reproach.

The session began with a flurry of shares as the women released pent-up emotions. There had been breakdowns and breakthroughs; sleepless nights as well as last-minute revelations; frustrations as well as rewards. Gill told them the best way to pay tribute to those experiences was to read their work aloud as if every word mattered.

"The rest of us will offer appreciative attention," he said. "Feedback is welcome, but not the main point. Who wants to go first?"

Morgan avoided Gill's gaze, but Andrea put up her hand and read with almost no dramatic inflection. She unfolded a scene of childhood bullying made worse by her parents' failure to act.

The language was precise: a staccato of hurts punctuated by the parents' silence. Good metaphors too. The piece was lean and well-structured. When she finished, Gill let the silence linger and then tapped his metal bowl twice.

"That was a tsunami of emotion delivered in a velvet glove," Jess offered, as the others murmured agreement.

A woman called Marion went next. Even with glasses, she found it hard to read since she had printed her story in ten-point font. They willed her through every painful word. A few more readings, and then it was Robin's turn. Her piece was light and had the cadence of a sermon. She described her first flailing steps as an artist and imagined a celestial review board giving a critique. It was a crowd pleaser first to last.

On that happy note, Gill called time and said they would hear the other readings tomorrow. He advised them to get a good night's sleep and not second guess their stories. It was good advice. Morgan had begun to wonder already if his writing was too dry or too earnest. No, he would trust Gill's advice.

He lingered in the vestibule in hopes of catching Eve; while he waited, he thumbed through the Book of Runes. When she walked past arm-in-arm with Jess and ignored him, he kept on reading to save face. It was then that he came to a page about the blank rune. Far from being a dud, the stone with nothing on it had real meaning. One sentence in particular stood out: 'This rune calls for no less an act of courage than an empty-handed leap into the void.'

9

Morning arrived at last. Morgan ate breakfast and went early to the session hoping to speak with Eve. When she trailed in late, more phantom than solid flesh, he was certain that something was wrong and had a vague sense of being punished.

The readings began with Lily, but Morgan's attention was fixed on Eve. Each aspect of Lily's life was mirrored, beat-for-beat, in Eve's anguished expressions. She kept her head down through the next few readings, but raised it again for Jess. Morgan noticed some subtle changes from the earlier draft. An argument with her father had been removed, and some of the more gruesome hospital scenes had been softened. Her voice sounded small in the room, as if she found the audience intimidating, but the piece still had a powerful impact.

"That was brave," Lily said. "Don't change a word."

"I think y'all could cut some hospital description."

Heads turned towards Savannah. There were murmurs of resistance and attempts to mitigate the critique, but Gill intervened and said it was a good observation.

"In a piece like that," he said, "you need to keep the tension high. Who's next?"

Eve put up her hand. She had changed out of her overalls and now wore a long, moss-green skirt. She took a swig from Jess's water bottle, reached into her basket with both hands and produced a large rock. She tucked the rock under the folds of her skirt and told them it was for grounding.

As she read, her hair fell like a curtain and half-concealed her face. Even so, Morgan could see the tension that ran down the side of her jaw; from time to time, she would stumble over a word or a phrase as if the letters had caught in her throat.

The content of the writing was new to him. Eve was at the bedside of an elderly man close to death. She described the room in minute detail and then moved on to the man. He lay in a slant of light, the air stagnant around him; as he drew in a deep and ragged breath, he reached out a skeletal hand for comfort. Eve took the hand and folded her angular body into the bed.

The story ended there; Gill struck the metal bowl, and the sound seemed to echo the man's passing. It was Robin, experienced in death, who acknowledged the grace of Eve's compassion. Others added their praise, but Morgan stayed silent. When the story had reached its climax, the only thing he felt was a stab of unacceptable jealousy

"We'll stop there," Gill said, after a pause. "You can take the afternoon off. You've done good work, and Gina has organized a beach trip as a surprise; there's a sign-up sheet in the kitchen. Go have some fun. Morgan and Savannah will read tonight as our grand finale."

Lunch was a good distraction - grilled haloumi with roast potatoes and green beans. Morgan retreated to a spot outside under the half-open kitchen window and ate to a soundtrack of the women dissecting the readings like carrion crow. He missed dessert, but Savannah surprised him with the gift of a brownie on a white plate.

"Does that mean I'm forgiven?" he asked.

"Don't push your luck," she replied.

She was giving the beach a miss; the sun was unkind to someone with her complexion. Besides, she needed time to put the finishing touches to her piece. Morgan detected nerves under her swagger. She wasn't an easy fit for this group; she alienated where she sought to belong.

Eve's name was not on the beach list either, but she appeared at the last minute and got into the front passenger seat of Gina's untidy van.

"I've had my sister's kids in here," Gina apologized, "so watch out for chewing gum."

Morgan toed discarded candy wrappers aside and got in next to Robin.

"Are you nervous about reading?" she asked. "It's hard going last. When I gave my sermons, I'd find a few friendly faces in the crowd and focus on them."

"But you weren't spilling your guts," Morgan said.

"Is that what you're going to do?" Eve asked, turning around in her seat to look at him.

"Not all of them, but enough."

Eve turned back and became engaged in a conversation with Gina about some of the more difficult guests they'd hosted. It struck him that she enjoyed gossip.

When they parked near the water, Eve took off her shoes and socks, rolled up her pant legs and claimed Robin as her walking partner. The two of them wandered off in a southerly direction, and Morgan trailed along behind.

The beach was littered with driftwood shelters and rocks piled into cairns. If he hadn't been following the two women, Morgan might have stopped to build something himself. When they paused to admire a tree-stump covered with shells, he fell to his knees and pretended to search for sand dollars.

Eve wore giant sunglasses that cast a shadow over her face. He could hear bits of their conversation about grief and rules around appropriate work clothing. Robin had always preached in slacks, while Eve had been censured for dressing in a way that was deemed too sensuous for the dying.

"As if it matters when you're dealing with life and death," Eve said, her voice rising. "If I gave pleasure to someone in the last hours of their life, then I'm glad."

They moved out of range and Morgan made no attempt to follow. He wondered what it would be like to have Eve at one's deathbed. Distracting, he thought. Even in overalls, she drew your eye. He turned towards the water and took off his shoes and socks then played in the shallows and skimmed stones. He managed two, three, four skips, but each time the embryonic waves swallowed his efforts. Tom's record had been nine, or so he claimed, but that was on a placid lake in Wisconsin in full summer.

When he grew bored of trying to beat Tom's record, he cut back towards the shore and sat down against a fallen tree. By now, the women were minute specks on the horizon. He removed his shirt and let his calves become fodder for whatever crawled in the sand. With eyes closed, he listened to the gulls as they fought over clams and then hurled them down to smash on the rocks.

When he woke, he was in shadow. Eve stood over him with her eyes still hidden behind glass.

"How long have you been there?" he asked.

"Long enough to watch you drool. Come on; it's time to go back. You've burned yourself," she added, touching the skin on his chest.

He scrambled to join her, but she was ahead of him and linked back up with Robin. The three of them rinsed sandy feet under the communal taps near the parking lot, and Eve used his shoulder for balance leaving her imprint on his tender skin.

The van ride back was peaceful. Several women had beach-swag, and Robin showed him a moon shell with a sprig of seaweed pressed into the end like a seal. He asked what she would do with her treasure, and she told him she would give it to her husband so he knew where she'd been.

Back at the site, bodies slithered out of the van and vanished, but Robin lingered. She was going to make tea, she said, and asked Morgan to join her. She brewed two mugs and added milk without asking. They sat together, looking out over the garden, while their pockets released trickles of sand.

"I overheard some of your conversation with Eve," Morgan said. "You seem to have a lot in common."

He waited, expectant, but Robin shook her head.

"Secrets of the confessional, I'm afraid. What about you? Anything to confess?"

"I'm not ready to go home," he admitted.

"What awaits you there?"

"Not much, to tell you the truth."

They watched as a woman dug into the earth with easy vigor. Her movements were rhythmic and precise. She was making a trench of some kind.

"A lot opens up on a retreat," Robin said, quietly. "When you return home, you might find that parts of your life no longer fit."

"What do you mean?" he asked.

"Just go slow. Recognize you are vulnerable. You need to be a little kinder to yourself."

Morgan took a long, last swallow of tea and said he needed to go and print his manuscript ahead of the reading. When he stood to leave, Robin wrapped her arms around him and held on for what seemed a long time.

"Something tells me you don't get too many of those," she said, as she released him.

Back in his cabin, Morgan slumped onto his bed and shed the rest of the sand. He didn't care; sleep was still elusive and out of his control; extra grit in the sheets would make little difference.

He opened his canvas bag, ready to add the printed pages, and noticed the sliver of card that Eve had slipped into his bag that night in her room. It was shaped like a bookmark and carried the imprint of her lips. He thought of Savannah and the napkin. Below the lips, Eve had written her message in green ink.

Shaped like a poem, her words recalled long-ago juvenile valentines he had received in school and pored over for days and weeks.

> To the quietly
> Mysterious Morgan
> whose flame-hair
> inspires poets and
> captivates women.
>
> I dreamed of you
> last night...
> We only got to
> second base, but
> the making-out
> was delicious.

10

Morgan shuffled his pages and prepared to read, but his mind kept straying back to Eve's story. Was it appropriate to be intimate with a dying man she barely knew? What about the man's family? What about professional distance? Was it typical of her to do something like that?

The sheets in his hand trembled, and he gripped them more firmly with both hands. He thought of the blank rune and the empty-handed leap into the void. This was it; no going back. He was about to reveal himself in front of these women. He would no longer be the dispassionate objective journalist; he would be the boy whose one true friend had been a dog.

Bodies leaned forward in his peripheral vision and Gill rested the tip of her pen on a blank sheet of paper. Morgan felt suspended - a vertigo of facts and feelings – before he plunged back into the house with his parents and with Sideways close at his heels. He was a boy again, running between need and loss.

His mouth felt dry and words trapped in the triangle of his throat. But he felt the deep holding silence of the room and it kept him safe. Then it was over. The bowl sounded.

When he looked up, several women were crying. Savannah mimed applause from across the room.

"Your hands shook through the entire reading," Lily exclaimed.

"Pent-up creativity," Gill observed. "There were no missteps there."

The comment, simple yet with an air of finality, seemed to silence the room. Morgan felt light-headed. By giving the story weight, he had simultaneously released a burden. But there was no time to dwell on his success. Now, it was Savannah's turn; she had saved herself for last.

The writing was good, and she had tamed the more outlandish parts of her story. She might play the part of the eccentric, but she was shrewd and knew what was marketable. When she had finished, there was a smattering of praise but nothing memorable from Gill; Morgan knew she would consider it insufficient applause.

"Incredible readings everyone; thank you," Gill said. "It's not easy to put yourself out there. Now it's time to bathe in the afterglow. I may join you at dinner tonight, but if not, I'll see you tomorrow for the wrap-up session."

No one wanted to move. Like children, they knew that the magic would end as soon as they left the room.

"Am I going to have to kick you out?" Gill laughed. "Okay, on your feet and hold hands in a circle. Each of you tell me one thing you've learned this week."

"You need a good, solid container for prose," Lilly mimicked Gill.

"Too many details kill a story; too few can do the same," Savannah called out.

"Use at least twelve-point font," Marion warned.

"Find a really young photo for the dust jacket," Morgan blurted, his hands sweaty.

Gill shouted with laughter and the circle broke apart in noisy celebration. Women hugged and exchanged the compliments they had kept in reserve. Then Morgan felt a hand in the small of his back.

"Your writing is so sure," Eve said, "like a good dance partner. I felt complete trust."

"I loved your piece too," he lied. "Such an unusual story. You've been quiet today," he added. "It's strange that we've barely spoken."

The hand flew away; he wished he'd kept things light.

"It's the longing," Eve whispered. "The longing is unbearable. Who knew?"

At dinner, most of the women released the tension they had carried for days, but Eve was withdrawn. She avoided Morgan's gaze and spoke mostly with Jess. Morgan knew that something was being asked of him, but what?

Wine appeared in short promiscuous tumblers. Savannah grew familiar and Morgan leaned away from her under the pretext of speaking with Robin. When Gill joined them for dessert, several women grew ostrich-necks and showered him with outlandish compliments. Only Eve and Jess, sequestered at the far end of the table, seemed immune. When Gill left, they followed his lead without bothering to say goodnight.

"To women writers everywhere," Lilly toasted. "May we rock the world and speak our truth."

"What about Morgan?" someone asked.

"To women writers and our honorary woman, Morgan," Lily amended.

"Honorary woman, my ass," Savannah roared. "Give the man his balls."

The table cut up laughing, and Morgan stood with hands cupped at his groin. He said it was the perfect moment to retire. He left to a chorus of cat calls and Savannah accusing him of being a coward.

Out in the courtyard, he ran into Jess. She told him that Eve had gone to bed with a migraine. She was looking for pain meds and then needed to book a shuttle for the following day.

"I live in Tacoma, you know."

"I heard. I'd say we should get together, but with two kids, one husband, a part-time job and a single car, it's unlikely. That said, you're welcome to come to ours."

"I meant I could give you a ride tomorrow. You can let me know in the morning. No pressure."

"I'll check with Eve. I have to be home by the afternoon, but her flight isn't until early evening."

Women began to flow out of the kitchen with loud plans for the hot tub, so Jess said he'd better escape. He didn't offer to help with Eve; he was useless around sick people. He took a long route back to his cabin and spent the next half-hour sweeping his floor free of sand. When he lay down to sleep, his throat scratchy from the wine, he spent most of the night awake and listening to a dog howl its fury at being locked up outside.

At sunrise, Morgan splashed cold water on his face and tucked his hair behind his ears; in the mirror, he thought he resembled a bad Jesus. He packed quickly, dirty clothes in with clean, and left the owl's nest cabin with barely a backward glance.

In the courtyard, he stowed his bags in a corner and ate alone before the women were awake. At the first signs of movement, he walked down to the gathering space and contorted his body into a BackJack for the last time. While he waited, he put the final touches to his article about the retreat. It was a solid story, spiced with quotes from Savannah and with a generous depiction of Gill.

When the women filtered in, heavy with hangover, Gill arrived in a linen suit that was pretty enough for a night at the opera. He carried a stack of books, held away from his body, and began with formal thanks. He told them to keep writing and gave them a reading list with his own titles listed first.

"Now," he said, "each of you retrieve your object from the bowl and offer a few words about your experience and your ongoing writing plans."

With barely a hesitation, Morgan reached forward and grabbed his stone from the bowl. If he had learned one thing, it was the wisdom of going first. Any of these women were capable of setting the bar too high.

"I'm not good at this kind of thing," he said. "But I've uncovered stories I didn't know were in me. As for the future, writing is my day job, so there's no escape."

He sat back and slipped the stone into his pocket. His heart felt ungovernable; it was hard to listen to the others, but Robin's checkout moved him the most. She held the painting against her chest and spoke about fellowship and how much it meant to be seen as a writer and an artist.

Eve spoke next. She compared writing practice to the demands of a jealous lover: no amount was ever truly enough. She was afraid of the retreat ending and didn't know what lay ahead. After that, Morgan heard nothing.

The bowl became empty which meant Gill must have removed his pen some time before. Either he hadn't trusted his own process, or he hadn't trusted them. As he ordered them to write their hearts out, Gill clasped the willing hands of the women on either side of him and raised them into the air.

The room became haphazard. Some women had travel deadlines and rushed for the door; others swapped contact details and promised to stay in touch. A subset grabbed copies of Gill's books and formed a line. Morgan lurked on the fringes of this group and stepped forward at the same time as Eve.

"Who's first?" Gill asked, seeming amused.

Eve planted a soft kiss on Gill's left cheek, handed him a bouquet of wilting flowers and described the retreat as 'immeasurably precious'. He signed her book with a flourish and told her to keep the faith.

"Last but not least," Gill said, turning to Morgan. "Shall I sign the book to you or someone else?"

"To me."

"You're right," Gill said, looking at the photograph on the dust jacket. "Absurdly young. But young or old, Colin was brilliant with the camera."

"It's perfect for a book cover," Morgan agreed.

"Thank you for sticking this out," Gill said, handing the book back much too fast to have written anything original. "I think you shifted from sceptic to believer over the ten days. Is that fair?"

Morgan nodded. He lacked Eve's courage for an intimate gesture; anyway, he had no idea what would be appropriate man-to-man.

"Something significant happened here," Gill continued. "Trust the process and see where it leads."

Morgan waited until the room was almost empty and then opened the book to the inscription page. The handwriting was slanted and old-fashioned: 'Believe in the power of story; trust where it takes you. Story is the thread that will carry you home.'

Eve looked over his shoulder. He asked if her inscription was the same, but she shook her head. She didn't elaborate, and they left the building together. They walked away from the main path and onto a wooded trail. Halfway along, Eve noticed a crude doll tucked into some tree branches. She started to lift it out then changed her mind and pushed it further into the crevice. It resembled a peasant woman with drawn-on features and a scrap of cloth over its head.

"It's creepy," said Morgan.

"She's beautiful," corrected Eve. "Almost alive. I wonder who made her."

"It's just a few twigs and a bit of old lumber. Anyone could have done it."

"But not anyone would."

They walked on and came to the building used for overflow guests. It was open, but the entrance hall was musty as if no one had stayed there in months. A visitors' book, open on a wooden table, showed a blank page. Eve stuck her head inside the nearest door and then opened it wide.

"Look! It's set up like Virginia Woolf's study. There's a picture of her on the desk and those are some of her books. It's a room of her own; but what discipline you would need to sit and write for hours. I wish I had that."

She examined the books and then sank down on a single bed that ran along one of the walls. She drew her legs up and tipped over to lay on her side. Morgan eased out his phone and took one, two, three photographs.

"What are you doing?" Eve asked.

"Fixing a memory."

"Don't. Anyway, you should have asked my permission. Come, lie down here with me."

Face-to-face, she ordered another photograph, and he held the phone as far away as his arm allowed. His breath felt shallow and complicated, as if wool had invaded his lungs. He could see the twitch and dance of Eve's eyelid veins and he leaned closer just as her eyes flew open. She shoved a powerful hand against his chest.

"Were you trying to kiss me? Why?"

"I don't know…instinct, I suppose," he stuttered.

"Instinct," she repeated flatly, still pinning him with her palm as if he was a moth.

At that precise moment, Morgan felt something heavy move from Eve's chest and enter his own - a hard deposit, a direct transmission, something that linked them in burden. Then her hand relaxed and she pushed him away.

"Jess will wonder where I am," she said. "And I need to finish packing."

"Can I give you a ride to the airport?" he begged. "So that we have more time."

"What's the point? The end result will be the same".

11

Eve's tone had conveyed resignation. Morgan thought about that as he loaded her luggage into his truck. When he was done, she kicked one of his back tires and asked if they would make it to the airport in one piece.

"We'll make it," he assured her. "This truck has survived plenty of Wisconsin winters."

"Tell that to a Minnesotan," Eve shot back.

"You're from Minnesota?"

"Imported."

"Like a fine wine," added Jess, as she joined Eve on the narrow back seat.

"One of you could ride up here with me," he said, but the two women only laughed. "Fine," he said, adjusting the rear-view mirror to focus on Eve. "I'll play chauffeur, but the partition stays open."

"Okay by us," Eve said. "For the record, I was dragged kicking and screaming to the Midwest."

"That's not what you told me," Jess protested.

"Poor Luke; I like to cast him as the villain."

Luke. A man with the power to drag Eve to a place she did not belong. He had become real, and Morgan was glad, suddenly, that Eve had stopped the kiss.

The drive to the ferry felt interminable. His passengers were giddy with freedom, and Savannah was the easy butt of their jokes. His own goodbye with her had been tender. Savannah had cornered him on the bridge and told him that she wanted to stay in touch.

"Not many people get me," she had said. "Admit it, I grew on you in the end."

He did admit it, and she hugged him like a perfumed boa constrictor and thrust a business card into his hand. She warned him to be careful of his heart, and he pretended not to understand. What would she think if she knew he was giving Eve and Jess a ride?

When they reached the dock, they joined a line of vehicles waiting for the ferry. Eve and Jess left the truck and sauntered off arm-in-arm. He spotted them minutes later sitting on a bench licking ice cream cones. Jess used her whole mouth, while Eve flicked at the melting mass with a lizard-like tongue.

When engines went from idle to engaged, he honked his horn twice and had already released the handbrake and eased forward when the women ran back. Eve called him unchivalrous, but he ignored her and focused on the men and women in hi-viz guiding him onto the boat.

"Let's go up on deck and enjoy our last glimpse of the island," Eve cried. "It will all be a distant memory soon; we'll wonder if this trip even happened."

They joined a line of passengers and climbed up the narrow stairs, passing through a covered cabin and out into the open air. The wind whipped their jackets, and Jess leaned back over the railing and flung out her arms.

"Titanic moment," she screamed, as Eve took a photograph.

"Take one of the two of us, will you?" she asked, passing Morgan her phone.

He studied them on screen: Jess with her mothering body and Eve so slender she was bent by the force of the wind. He took a wide shot then zoomed in on their faces.

A man offered to snap the three of them, but Eve shook her head and retrieved the phone.

"I'm not ready to go home," she confided, when Jess went inside to buy water. "Not after what happened."

"Technically, nothing happened."

"You know what I mean."

Jess returned, and the three of them played a game of spotting birds and animals in the water. Jess claimed she saw a porpoise, and Morgan counted at least four ducks lost immediately in the boat's wake.

"I think my migraine is back," Eve complained.

"It's the dread of return," Jess stated. "A malady that afflicts wives and mothers."

They were silent after that, until the loudspeaker announced a ten-minute warning and they went back to the truck. On the mainland, Jess moved to the front seat, while Eve stretched out on the back. The boat ride had made them sober.

"Left, and then a sharp right," Jess commanded, once they were close to the suburbs. "That's us next to the Masonic Hall."

"Great location," Morgan commented. "You're lucky to have quiet streets and a view of the water."

"Developers make offers, but we'd be priced out of the neighborhood if we agreed."

"Are we here?" Eve asked, clawing up to sitting. "Are you the mansion or the cute one with the red door?"

Before Jess could answer, the red door opened and a heavy-set man appeared with a child clamped under each arm. He held them until Jess reached the lawn, then they flew like slingshots into their mother's arms.

"They make it look easy, don't they?" remarked Eve, taking Jess's spot in the front of the truck. "From the outside anyway. But it's never the whole story."

"Did you ever want kids?" he asked.

"That's a complicated question," Eve replied.

They made small talk after that, but as they got near to the off-ramp for the airport, Morgan felt a rush of nausea and regretted the wasted time.

"There are so many things I don't know about you," he blurted.

"Of course. But we may never see each other again," Eve said, quietly. "I'd like to, but we live so far apart. We could be pen pals, I suppose."

"Pen pals," he echoed. "Should I drop you off or come into the terminal?"

"Drop me off," Eve said. "That way I leave you and not the other way around."

He pulled up to the curb and helped Eve with her bags. A cop caught his eye and pointed to No Waiting sign.

"So, this is it," Morgan said.

"This is it," she agreed, placing her hands on his shoulders. "I'm glad we met."

Her expression was at odds with her words, and he felt a twinge of anticipated loss that made him pull her closer.

"Move it on, buddy," said the cop.

Back in the truck, he watched Eve walk through the sliding glass doors towards check-in. The cop, out of patience now, rapped on the hood and Morgan lurched off only to circle the airport one more time.

Two hours later, he had just stepped out of a hot shower when thirty bright seconds of Bruce Springsteen burst from his phone. He let it go to voicemail, dried off with one of the ancient towels Kim had discarded, and opened a beer Savannah-style. Then his phone rang again.

"Yup," he said, knowing that if it was Margaret, she would abhor his casual tone.

"Finally," a voice said.

"Who is this?"

"Forgotten so soon? I'm mortified."

"Faith?"

"I'm losing faith right now…"

"Eve?"

"He does remember! I missed my flight."

"How the hell did you manage that?"

Eve ignored the question and asked if he wanted to keep her company while she waited for the next flight which wasn't until the early hours of the morning.

"Don't take this the wrong way, Eve," he said, "but I don't want to slog back to the airport. I only just got out of the shower."

But Eve wasn't at the airport. Fifteen minutes later, Morgan pulled up to the Ukulele Café on the edge of his own zip code. Country music twanged from speakers and the café's front window showed a tasteless collage of musical decals. Nice choice, Eve. He found her on a mock leather sofa sitting next to a tubby man with crooked teeth and facial stubble.

"There you are," she said. "I was just telling Angel how we met."

"Happy to meet friend of Eve," the man said.

Morgan wondered if this was how the evening would go – the three of them in an awkward trio exchanging two-syllable words. But Eve whispered something to Angel who jumped to his feet and gave a funny little bow before he scuttled off to the exit.

"What did you say to him?" Morgan asked.

"I told him you get jealous. He understood that very well. It's true, isn't it? You were a little jealous when you found I wasn't alone."

Morgan grabbed a menu off a nearby table and studied it closely, but Eve touched his arm and said they wouldn't be staying. She pointed to a basket at her feet and said she wanted to have a picnic down by the water.

"It's not scenic," he objected. "This is an old port town. And you still haven't told me what happened. How did you miss your flight?"

But Eve had gathered her coat and backpack and was headed to the door.

"Where's the rest of your luggage?" he asked, picking up the basket and trailing along behind.

"My bags are checked onto that other flight," she assured him. "You're quite safe; you can relax."

He took her to the only place he knew. As they drove past rusted tankers and a restaurant boasting the 'best local fish in a mile', he told her he preferred his fish without the aftertaste of diesel. She laughed and he felt at ease again; it didn't matter why she had missed her flight, it only mattered that she had wanted to be with him.

They parked where the road ended under a sign for a walking trail. It was too early for night lights and too late for perfect vision, so they walked close together while the bats or birds swooped past them and flew over the water. When the trail ended, Morgan scrambled partway up the bank and then held a hand down for Eve. The feel of skin-on-skin made him dizzy.

They found a bare spot between two trees that was almost level, but the ground was damp and he wished he had brought a blanket from the truck. He made a makeshift seat with his jacket while Eve began to pull things from her basket. She apologized about the plastic, but said she'd made up for that with a bottle of wine.

"When did you have time to do all his?" he asked, taking the bottle and unscrewing the cap.

"Angel took me to a deli; he was my cab driver, by the way. He thought my plan was romantic."

"It is," Morgan said, and poured wine into two plastic beakers.

For a while, they sipped wine and tore off chunks of bread to dip into humous, but then Eve asked about the rustling sounds coming from the bushes.

"Could be squirrels or chipmunks," he told her. "But homeless people sleep up here too."

She moved closer, and the evening settled around them like a dog turning in its basket before landing with a satisfied sigh.

Lamps came on near the harbor, and he could just make out Eve's profile as she whispered her confession to the evening air.

"I wasn't ready to say goodbye," she admitted.

It was easy then to let his head touch hers and to search out her lips, salty from olives. And when Eve shifted her body down, Morgan felt the full mysterious length of her. He told himself not to rush. He stroked the side of her face and traced a line down her neck into the low spot between her collar bones where the skin was almost papery. He moved lower still and grazed a thumb on the furthest rise of one breast.

Eve stiffened and then relaxed, so he loosened two buttons on her shirt and landed small kisses at the edges of her bra. Pleasure bumps rose on her skin, and he eased the lace of her bra aside and reached with his tongue. Her nipple was soft, like the inside of a peach, but firmed as he worked in small, tight circles; he pulled with his teeth, the way an animal might pluck a berry, and Eve clasped his head and drew him back to face-level.

"What are we doing?" she asked.

The question made him pull away, and the move unsettled them both. A water bottle went flying and when he tried to catch it, something hard and metallic fell into the bushes some distance away.

"Shit; that's my phone," he said.

"I have to pee," Eve declared, buttoning her shirt and moving up and away from him.

He got down on all fours and began to move gingerly down the slope. As he felt with his hands, earth lodged under his finger nails and a thorn pricked the soft flesh below his right thumb. Somewhere above him, liquid hit the ground in a long, strong stream.

"I'm peeing like a racehorse," Eve cried.

Then his hand stuck something hard, and a tsunami of relief flooded his body. He retrieved his phone and clawed his way back to Eve.

"All of my work contacts are on this phone," he explained, his stomach still metallic. "Zoe would have killed me. I can't believe I was so stupid."

"But there's no harm done, is there? You found the phone."

She had begun to pack the basket, saying she was cold and needed coffee. When they scrambled down the bank, he held onto her hand, but she snatched it back as soon as they hit level ground.

In the half-light, the trail looked desolate with old discarded food wrappers and mangled to-go cups. He tried to think of a cheerful café, but the one he chose had a closed sign in the window. Eve got out of the truck and tapped on the glass. A kid with a broom unlocked the door and said there was hot water for tea but no coffee as he'd already turned off the machine.

While Eve made her drink, Morgan sought out the restroom on the second floor. He climbed a narrow set of stairs and went along a landing lined with old movie seats that bore a century's worth of dust. Eve was perched on one of these when he came out.

"Such beauties," she said. "They just need love and attention."

The tea tasted like sawdust, so Eve hid her cup under one of the seats and they left the boy to his sweeping. In the truck, she told him the boy's name was Shane and he was studying to be a nurse.

"He'd better brush up on his hygiene then; that restroom is a killer."

She laughed and turned to face him in the soft glow of streetlights that filtered into the front of the truck.

"Your hair gives off a kind of aura in this light," she said. "Promise me that you will always keep it long."

12

The second airport drop-off held more promise than the first. Eve suggested they find a quiet corner of a parking lot where they could wait out the next few hours. They sat huddled together under his blanket.

"Why did your parents name you Eve?" he asked "It's a tough name for a girl."

"Not that Eve," she laughed. "My mother was reading a book when she was pregnant with me, and the main character was Evelyn; she shortened that to Eve."

"Too bad," he joked, touching her thigh.

"And the Evelyn in question was a man," she added, staying his hand. "Some British book." She lifted his hand to her cheek. "What we did earlier felt complicated."

"Then why did you call? What did you expect?"

"I don't know. I'm sorry. It's messed up; I'm messed up. I need you to be patient. Can you do that?"

When he didn't answer, she took his face in her hands. Slowly, carefully, she kissed him as if exploring every blood vessel and nerve ending in his lips. And then she got out of the truck.

For the second time, Morgan watched her walk away across a parking lot and through sliding glass doors. Her backpack, half-on and half-off, made her arms appear bound. He wanted to run after her, settle the pack more comfortably, say something that would link them together. But he let her disappear with no reassuring sign.

That failure would haunt him for days. He had no idea if the airport scene was a final act played out between them, or the first deposit on a relationship not yet begun. He heard nothing from Eve; he didn't even know if she got safely home. In the absence of any communication, all he could do was throw himself into his work and try to limit thoughts of Eve to only once or twice a day.

Zoe loved his article. On his first day back at work, she had rapped on his desk and said she'd consider a follow-up to see how the writers were doing. That, at least, would give him a legitimate reason to contact Eve. He'd already sent the entire group a link to his article, but only Robin and Lily had bothered to respond.

A welcome distraction came in the form of a letter from his mother. She had sent a card for his birthday, sourced from the stash in her kitchen dresser since it was the same design as the year before. A follow-up, hand-written letter was unusual.

He skipped through the complaints about his father missing meals and spending too much time in his shed, but he lingered on the revelation that Tom had sent Mother's Day flowers. It was easy when you had a secretary to remind you about key dates. A smattering of local gossip followed; close to the end, he found the real purpose for the letter. There was 'news' Margaret wanted to share with the whole family.

Unable to penetrate the mystery, since his mother offered no clues, he called his sister, Faith. Together, they speculated about what might merit a family sit-down. It could be something medical, or a monetary decision, or maybe the trans-Atlantic cruise his father had dreamed of for as long as Morgan could remember.

"I guess we'll find out in August, when we're all at the farm," Faith said, giving up the game.

"August?" Morgan queried. "Remind me, Sis."

"Does a 45th wedding anniversary ring any bells?"

"Oh, shit. I'd forgotten about that."

"Don't worry. I'm going to bring the kids to visit you this summer, so we can shop together for a gift. But talking of weddings, do you know Kim had the nerve to invite me to her engagement party. Can you believe that?"

"You can go if you want; she's your friend."

Her reply, coming back to him in the middle of the night, had been touchingly vehement. Nothing on God's green earth would induce her to go to the party, unless Morgan needed a spy. He wished he could have told her about Eve, but what was there to tell? Eve was off limits. She was married. It was time to move on.

But moving on wasn't easy. Zoe kept banging on about a follow-up article and then said she wanted a longer interview with Savannah.

"And what about the woman with the rock?" she asked. "What was that for again?"

"Grounding," Morgan said, regretting that he had shared that detail.

"That's it. Imagine if I went along to an editors' meeting lugging a great big rock. It would be worth it just to see their expressions. What else have you got?"

"I've been thinking about a new feature: Stories from a Street Corner - a literal street corner. Like a microcosm of Seattle."

Zoe sucked in her cheeks and adjusted the pen she kept behind one ear.

"Maybe. Do a trial run, but don't limit yourself to one street corner; we can fudge a little. And make it up-beat; advertisers want positive news of their city."

As she peeled off his desk, Rob appeared waving a pale green envelope which Zoe plucked from his hand.

"It's for you," she told Morgan. "Looks personal." She smelled the envelope. "Definitely personal."

"Aren't you going to open it?" Rob enquired.

"Not at work," Morgan said, primly, putting the envelope into his bag.

When Rob left, he pulled the envelope out and studied it below the level of his desk. On the back seal, a faint imprint of lips confirmed the sender; when he slit the seal, a shower of lavender fell onto the floor. Next time, if there was a next time, he would open Eve's letters at home.

She had written from a park bench somewhere near her house. In the first paragraph, she painted a scene of spindly aspens and wilted ferns stretched beyond capacity. The second paragraph caught him off guard. Eve missed him. The previous night, at the exact same moment that she saw him in a dream, the wind blew her front door open: *As if you were there*, she wrote.

He read that paragraph several times before moving on to the second page. Eve was now on the steps of her local grocery store having *escaped the chaos of home*. It was evening, and all she had on under her long coat was a pair of flannel pajamas. On the way home, she stopped at a dimly-lit bar where a young man offered to buy her a drink. He had stared unabashedly at her breasts, and she had been forced to rebuff him.

Morgan gathered the lavender seeds and threw them in the trash. He returned Eve's letter to its envelope and walked out of the office and down to the corner store. When he opened the letter for the second time, he was under a maple tree and onto his third cigarette. He smoothed the pages and read the letter again. Then, he took out his phone and called Eve.

When Eve picked up, she said it was a bad time and she would have to call him later. The call came as he was riding the light rail home. He turned to the window and whispered his thanks for her letter.

"Your descriptions were so vivid," he said. "I was there on the bench and the steps of the grocery store."

"But not in the bar?" Eve challenged.

"You've set the bar high," he said, ignoring her jibe.

"It's not a competition, Morgan. Don't over-think this. I have to go now; duty calls."

For the next several hours, Morgan over-thought and then started work on his reply. Well past-midnight, he had only a single page to his credit. He'd described his apartment 'post-Kim', using the term the way one might say 'post-apocalypse'. Would Eve find that funny? He added an anecdote from work and a description of a couple who'd been arguing about sex on the light rail.

He slept late, even for a Saturday, and lingered over his shower and shave. At noon, he consumed two fried eggs with toast along with three mugs of black coffee since he'd run out of milk. The rest of the day yawned ahead of him. He could go to the park for frisbee or join a barbecue with the few friends Kim had left him. Choices upon choices, and behind them all, the hum of Eve's presence and anxiety about his letter.

He needn't have worried. When Eve sent another note, one week later, there was no mention of what he had written. When he opened the envelope, at home this time, a shower of gold stars fell on his kitchen table along with a postcard of a punk band blowing bubbles. Eve had scrawled *I'm forever blowing* on the back.

Her letter was written on an old evaluation form from her local library. She included a scathing review of the questionnaire but confessed to a soft spot for the librarian who was fresh out of school and already blessed with a comb-over; apparently, he deserved pity more than critique. It was the strangest letter Morgan had ever received. There was no content at all that related directly to him.

13

Summer careened forward like a horse without a rider. Work was busy, Eve continued to write her strange letters, and Faith changed summer plans more than once. She was supposed to visit Morgan in June, but then the kids got flu and Jerry planned a family trip to Nebraska. She would need weeks to recover from that, and she would have to civilize him all over again.

The only real constant in Morgan's life during this time was his work. Savannah had agreed to an interview, but only if Morgan came and did it in-person. Zoe accepted the long-distance trip in theory, as long as Morgan was willing to generate a series of stories along the way for the Thanksgiving or Christmas edition. He would also have to write something about Savannah in the meantime to keep her fresh in readers' minds - a teaser campaign in anticipation of the longer piece. He promised to come up with something snappy.

When Faith fixed her third and definite date to visit, Morgan got an almost simultaneous announcement from Eve out of the blue. She was coming to see Jess; they had shared writing since the retreat and wanted to collaborate on a project. Did he want to see here while she was in Seattle?

"No expectations," she warned, "and there can't be anything physical between us. I'm saying this now, so we know where we stand."

"I get it," he told her. "You're a married woman. Strictly hands off."

"But not too hands off. Not unnaturally hands off. I'll call you again when I know more."

Eve's visit was slow to materialize. She needed to check with Luke; her work got busy; prices rose and the airline website crashed. It was only when she sent confirmation of her flight times that he noticed her visit coincided with Faith's.

As the time drew near, he tried to anticipate each woman's schedule and needs. Faith would be with him for five nights, and her focus would be shopping and tourist attractions. Eve would be in town Friday through Monday, but her exact schedule was dependent on Jess.

In order to maximize his chances of seeing Eve, he went early to the airport and loitered near the manacled carts in the baggage claim area. He spied her one floor above and joined the up-escalator just as she caught one going down. For a moment, it looked as if they would pass each other in comic mistiming, but Morgan jumped back.

"You didn't tell me you were coming to the airport," Eve exclaimed, arriving on his level.

She was thinner than before and looked at sea in her faded jeans and corduroy shirt; he noticed her hair was at the end of a dying cycle. They embraced and lingered in each other's arms.

"It is so good to see you," Morgan exhaled. "How are you? You seem…"

"Frayed at the edges?"

"I was going to say tired."

They stepped aside for a chubby individual who was sweating profusely and had two cumbersome suitcases balanced on his cart. Eve's bag, a green duffel, emerged from the conveyor belt and seemed equally heavy. Morgan had to drag it off the belt with both hands.

"Books," Eve explained, when he asked what was in there. "Resources to work with Jess. She just texted, by the way. She's driving around outside. I should go."

"Call me," he said.

At arrivals, he sat with closed eyes and re-lived the exquisite sensation of hugging Eve until small hands shook him awake.

"You guys have grown," Morgan exclaimed. "How old are you now - eight?"

"Ten!" said Zach, rising to the bait. "But I'm half-an-inch taller than Bella."

"Are you sure about that?"

Zach looked ready to burst, until Faith explained that Uncle Morgan was teasing.

"He's taller," declared Bella, "but I'm smarter."

"Tall or smart, it's great to see you," he declared.

The twins stayed clasped to his legs as he took over the job of wheeling his sister's luggage. There were a suspicious number of bags.

"One is practically empty," Faith explained. "It's called revenge shopping."

"Is Jerry still in trouble?"

"Nebraska was hell. One of his brothers couldn't drink, so we all had to go dry."

"Poor sis. Robbed of your tried and tested method for surviving the rednecks."

That was the extent of their confidences, since the kids talked non-stop on the drive back to his apartment. Within minutes of their arrival, the living room was littered with toys and comics, and for the first time in months it felt like a home. Although no amount of mess could hide bare walls and dying plants.

"It's a miracle you're alive," Faith said, closing his fridge door. "I assume we'll eat out most of the time?"

"As long as it's on Jerry's dime."

She punched his arm and asked why he had never learned to cook.

"Mom used to kick me out of the kitchen, remember? I never had a chance."

"In your defense, I found out-of-date chicken nuggets in the freezer. With any luck they'll poison the kids."

"Did you hear that?" Morgan asked, as he joined the twins on the pull-out sofa. "Your days are numbered. We had better make the most of our time."

But mid-way through their bout of play-fighting, his phone rang and the twins fell about laughing.

"That's a rock classic," he admonished, taking the call to his bedroom and emerging a short while later in a hoodie and jeans.

"Going somewhere?" Faith asked.

"A work thing," he said. "I'm so sorry."

"Are you sure it's not a hot date?" she quizzed, and the twins took up the chant of 'hot date, hot date', until he smothered them with a pillow.

Faith had brought her own wine, so he found her a glass and dug a corkscrew out of the junk drawer, casting a quick look at his reflection in the window over the sink.

"You look fine," Faith told him. "I'd date you."

He drove the forty minutes to Olympia with a dry mouth and fingers tapping the steering wheel. The sports bar was easy to find, but the barman was deep in a heated conversation about a late-stage baseball game and it took a while to get served. Eve and Jess were several glasses in when he made it to their table.

They were locked in a discussion on marriage and barely looked up when he slid into the booth next to Eve. She squeezed his hand, but then she turned back to Jess and commiserated about a never-ending pile of laundry and the loneliness of having kids.

"I'm sorry," she said, when Jess went to the restroom.

"She needs to unload. Poor Morgan. It's enough to put you off marriage for life."

"What are you love birds discussing?" Jess asked, when she got back.

"Love birds?" Eve repeated. "We're just friends."

"I was there, remember?" Jess laughed. "I'm not judging. A relationship like yours might actually help a marriage. God knows it isn't easy."

They talked as if he wasn't there; they talked as if he was expendable, useful only as he served the larger cause of Eve's marriage. He bought drinks, took away empties, and joined in the sports conversation at the bar. Only in the final few minutes did he get confirmation from Eve that they could meet again during her visit.

"Who zapped your happy tree?" Faith asked, when he got home.

"I'm just tired," he said, grabbing a beer from the fridge and then changing his mind. "In fact, I'm off to bed. Did the twins stay up long?"

"Out like lights twenty minutes after you left."

"Rascals. It's good to have you all here. Breakfast out tomorrow?"

Faith gave a thumbs up but said the inquisition wasn't over; she knew perfectly well his errand hadn't been for work. Morgan smiled and hugged her goodnight.

When the twins surfaced the next morning, they were unable to agree about a breakfast location. They had just given their blessing to a pancake place when Morgan got a text from Eve. Jess needed family time, so she'd made her escape. Could he come to the Ukulele Café?

"Change of plans everyone," he announced.

"Why?" pouted Bella. "I want pancakes."

"Trust me," he said, "they're a dime a dozen, and there's only one Ukulele Café. You'll love this place."

"A sudden inspiration?" asked Faith.

"Exactly. A brain-bomb."

But when they arrived, Zach called the pictures on the window dumb, and Faith whispered that it looked like something she'd find in northern Wisconsin.

"Appearances can be deceptive, Sis. The coffee's great and the menu looks interesting."

"You've never even eaten here?" Faith wailed.

Despite appearances, the café was doing a brisk business, and they waited five minutes to be seated. The kids, unable to shift gear, ordered pancakes while Morgan played safe with a fry-up and Faith chose the Orchestral Omelet with potato strings.

"They've taken the music motif a bit far, haven't they?" she complained. "Will the pancakes be guitars?"

"Will they, Mom? Will they?" asked Bella, tuned to adult asides.

Morgan diverted her attention by pointing out the play area near the back of the room. He walked the twins over there and began a game of plastic ten-pin bowling while he scanned the room for Eve. He found her, tucked behind a coffee display and reading a book.

"I saw you come in," she said.

"I had to get everyone settled," he explained. "I'm here with my sister and kids."

"I didn't think you'd acquired a wife and family."

"Funny. We're just going to have breakfast and then I'll be all yours."

"I'll join you, unless you want me to stay hidden?"

He did, of course, but there was no way of saying that without seeming rude, and Eve was already on her feet.

14

"Funny thing," Morgan called out, as they got near to Faith. "I was playing with the kids, and I ran into Eve. She was at the writing retreat."

The women sized each other up and shook hands. Faith was a good two inches taller and showed the solidity of her Wisconsin genes. Eve, willowy and slight, appeared translucent as she placed tapered fingers into Faith's meaty palm.

"You're not what I expected," Faith confessed.

"Why would you expect anything?"

"My brother made cryptic comments about middle-aged women at the retreat."

"Ungenerous," Eve reproached.

The twins had followed them to the table, curious about this newcomer who crouched down to be on their level. Bella was fascinated by Eve's ringlets, while Zach managed a shy smile. Both made room for her to sit between them at the table.

"My sister has kids," Eve explained. "Her youngest is still a baby. In my opinion, the back of a baby's neck is the most exquisite scent in the world."

"I know what you mean," Faith agreed, warmly. "And

they grow up so fast. Do you have kids of your own?"

Eve shook her head. She signaled the waiter and asked for a fresh coffee along with a bran muffin.

"So, you and Morgan got to know each other at the retreat?" Faith persisted.

"Know might be a bit strong. But a shared process creates a certain intimacy. I'm friends with Jess who was also on the retreat. I'm staying with her, but she's tied up with family today."

"Morgan hasn't said much about his experience."

"Hasn't he? I'd call it life changing."

"Food's here," Morgan announced, grateful for the distraction. "Let's chow down."

The pancakes were indeed shaped like miniature guitars. Bella refused to eat, at first, because they were so pretty. Conversation drifted towards a playful comparison of midwestern winters, and Morgan almost relaxed. But when Faith's cab arrived to take the family shopping and he walked her outside, she dug him in the ribs.

"Enjoy time with your friend," she said. "We'll be gone most of the day, so the apartment's all yours. I've promised the kids a Big Mac and a movie."

"Don't say it like that; she's married."

"Is she now? Then you'd better be careful. But no kids. I wonder what the story is there."

"Why does there have to be a story?" he asked.

"Just be careful," Faith repeated.

When Morgan did not return immediately, Eve joined him on the sidewalk.

"I was a hit with the kids," she observed, "but I think big sister disapproves."

"Let's not talk about her. Do you want more coffee or shall we make tracks?"

They glanced back at their table where a waiter had begun to sweep crumbs and dab at rivulets of syrup.

"Make tracks," they said, in unison.

They walked several blocks, past a convenience store with boarded-up windows and a row of ranch-style homes. One block more, and feral front yards gave way to manicured lawns and independent shops. A craft store caught Eve's attention, and she was soon wrist-deep in buttons and beads. Morgan watched from a position near the door.

When she held up a bracelet of beads strung on leather with a questioning look, he said he wasn't really into jewelry. Her hand fell and she moved on to the register where she paid for the bracelet and joked with the woman at the till. Morgan's head throbbed from the glare of shiny objects and fluorescent lights.

"Sorry," he mumbled, as they left. "Faith used to drag me to places like that."

"Poor Morgan. Such torture. But I thought it might feel different doing it with me."

"Okay, okay, I get it. I'm an ass."

"Yes, and I'm giving the bracelet to Jess."

They wandered on past shops where Eve stopped to smell soap or dab perfume on her skin. His headache worsened, and he steered her towards a public park where a band, stuck in the sixties, played familiar yet hard-to-name tunes. Eve put a dollar into the expectant hat and earned a wink from the lead singer. She was exalted from the exchange, but just as quickly her mood shifted down to quiet desolation.

"I should never have missed that plane," she said.

"Why did you?"

"I don't know. But now I'm lying to people I love."

"We should talk," he said. "My apartment isn't far. We've been walking in that direction."

"That's a bad idea. I told Jess I would get back in time to help with dinner."

"Please," he insisted. "Just for a little while. I'll be good."

Eve agreed, but only because the songs made her sad.

As they walked, Morgan held his breath; he was aware that one wrong word could make Eve change her mind. When he turned the key to his apartment, he made her enter first.

His place was cleaner than he expected. Faith must have stopped there on her way to the shops, since the kids' bed was a sofa again and the fridge had been stocked.

"Baba ghanoush and olive tapenade," Eve murmured. "I'd never have guessed."

The magic stopped short of his bedroom. Eve laughed when she saw the Captain Marvel sheets, and he was forced to explain that Marvel had been his childhood hero and Tom had bought the sheets as a joke. She sat down on the edge of the bed, and a tear leaked from her left eye caused by either sorrow or laughter. Morgan leant down and caught it with his lips.

If someone had asked, afterwards, how he rated their lovemaking, he'd have said neither good nor bad, neither satisfactory nor lacking. They had moved in a breathless contagion, and when it was over, they barely touched. He tried to cover them both with a blanket, but Eve threw it off and took her clothes into the bathroom.

"Jess expects me," she said, when she emerged fully dressed. "We need to leave. This was a mistake."

He attempted one last kiss, but Eve pulled out of range. She made him call a cab to take them back to the café where she'd left Jess's car. In the back seat of the cab, thrown together by a geography of worn seats, they held hands like teenagers after a bad prom.

"We should have tried harder to be friends," Eve said, avoiding his gaze.

"Don't you think this was inevitable?"

"It's all choice," came her flat reply.

"And what if I choose this?"

"It's not that simple."

She insisted on paying for the cab, hugged him briefly and then drove away. He watched the *Vote Democrat* sticker on the car's bumper vanish from sight. Back in the café, he drank coffee at the table where he'd discovered her earlier that day. He told himself he could smell her lavender scent and pretended the empty sugar packet was hers even though she didn't use sweetener.

By the time he returned home, Faith and the kids were back. He admired the toys they had bought and listened to their impressions of city sights he knew by heart. If Faith detected a lack of enthusiasm, she kept quiet and accepted his excuses about needing an early night.

But the morning brought little relief. When his alarm shrieked, Morgan buried his face in the pillows and searched for traces of Eve. When he found none, he blamed kids and popcorn, Faith and her Black Orchid perfume, himself for obliterating Eve's scent with his own sweaty aroma.

The day passed in a blur. Faith helped him buy an anniversary gift for his parents, a crystal pitcher his mother would place on the dresser and never use. He'd wanted to buy a set of antique silver scissors, a poignant reminder of the past, but Faith had deemed them too risky.

In the late afternoon, they went to the movies and he lost himself in buttery popcorn and a fight between good and evil starring a cast of animated ants. Afterwards, they ate burgers and fries and talked about which characters they liked the best.

The twins were a tonic, but away from their influence Morgan struggled to maintain his better mood.

"What's wrong with you?" Zoe asked, when he arrived late for work the next morning. "Are you sick or something?"

"He's sick for sure," Rob called, from the coffee machine. "Love-sick. Look at him. Moody for weeks and now he's got a face like a kicked puppy. Be gentle with him, he's obviously fragile."

"You're going to be fragile if you don't mind your own business," Zoe threatened.

Rob flashed a peace sign and slunk back to his desk, while Zoe tried a conciliatory tone.

"Look," she said, "you've got momentum going with your street corner idea and the retreat story. Don't screw things up. Get your head back in the game."

"On it," he said, trying to look keen, but Zoe had not finished with him.

"Set up a Q and A with the southern woman and let readers get to know her."

"The Muse Muses?"

"Cute. And I don't care if you have the worst hangover in the world, you need to be alert and productive whenever you're in the office."

"Got it. But it wasn't a hangover, my sister's in town and…"

"And next time you're late, you'll not only get the worse assignments, you'll buy the office coffee for a month."

15

Morgan stayed at his desk all day, but he achieved very little. The same was true the following day, even though he'd waved off his guests and could no longer claim them as a distraction. The truth was, he couldn't shake the idea that he'd blown his chances with Eve. He didn't even know how she felt about their lovemaking, beyond the cryptic comment about it being a mistake.

Days passed with no word from Eve, and Morgan concluded she had thrown him under the bus to focus on her marriage. He began to delay his arrival in the office each morning. Under the guise of research, he chose different cafés and sat where he could look onto the street. He sipped coffee, ate day-old pastries, and guessed at the professions of pedestrians based on their feet.

Brogues suggested dependable office worker; sneakers were casual laborers between jobs; bright red heels craved attention and made him think of Savannah. She had warned him about Eve, and she had been proved right. Eve was dangerous territory, and if he ever got around to writing his follow-up article, he would imbue Savannah with second sight.

At the start of another aimless Monday, he slid off a

warm stool and forced himself to engage with faces. His research had revealed an obvious fact: white, well-heeled professionals moved through the world with confidence, rarely stopping, and it was only musicians, veterans, and the homeless who hung out on street corners. Consequently, it might be a challenge to shape any stories that Zoe would like.

As he climbed the office stairs two at a time, he ran a conversation in his head which didn't lead to him being branded a failure. He was halfway to her office, when Rob waved an envelope and said he'd got mail.

"Give me that," Morgan almost shouted, snatching the letter out of Rob's hand.

"Chill out, man. I'm just doing my job."

He carried the envelope to the restroom, but it felt wrong to read Eve's words in that setting. All morning, he endured Rob's sideways glances, but when his friend left for lunch, he claimed the sofa set aside for clients and opened the envelope with care. But there were no cascades of lavender or stars, just a hand-written note.

Eve had been struggling with guilt since their last encounter. Guilt and a little shame. She had begun to see a therapist who specialized in psycho-sexual healing and worked with the body as well as the mind. Last week, she got wet on this woman's massage table, and she could report it was almost better than lovemaking. She begged him not to take this personally. Being away from him felt like a drought; she longed to feel the imprint of his body.

His relief was immense. Those last lines were all that he needed. Eve missed him; being away was like being in a drought; she longed to feel the imprint of his body.

Back at his desk, Morgan researched Madison hotels and wondered if Eve would prefer something flashy or more in the budget line. He opted for a Long Stay that was close to the highway yet a safe distance from the farm. It came with a kitchen and living area, but it wouldn't blow a hole in his wallet.

Morgan booked a double room and then wiped his search history clean. When he went to see Zoe in the late afternoon, he had two street-stories ready to pitch and ideas about how to downplay the homeless angle. But Zoe surprised him; she was happy to see him back on track and said even charities needed advertising and he could write the stories as he pleased. He used the moment to ask her for a few days off for his parents' anniversary in late August, and he promised excellent copy in return.

That evening, he called Margaret and confirmed his attendance at the anniversary dinner but said he would not be sleeping at the farm. Did she mind? Margaret ignored his question and prattled on about napkins and place settings. When he said the supper club would take care of details, she complained he was just like his father.

"Promise me you will look presentable for the dinner," she begged. "A suit and tie would be nice, and is it too much to expect short hair?"

"Goodbye, mother," he said, hanging up and dialing Eve right away.

She answered on the second ring, but she made him wait while she parked her car; he heard the handbrake engage and the click of a seatbelt release.

"You want me to come to your parents' wedding anniversary?" she repeated.

"Not exactly. I want you to come and spend time with me around that event. If we see each other, even for a day, I know we will feel better."

"Is that what you want?" Eve asked. "A day?"

It was not. He wanted days strung together and nights in a hotel with a 'Do Not Disturb' sign and twenty-four-hour room service. Most of all, he wanted Eve's undivided attention focused on him.

"I'm trying so hard to keep things together," she said, sounding desperate. "Luke's trying too. I don't know if I can do this to him."

"Don't decide now. Just think about it."

"I have to go. I only came out to buy coffee. I'm barely eating. If you saw me, you'd be concerned."

"Just think about it," Morgan repeated.

"I'll probably think of nothing else."

When confirmation arrived in his mailbox, it came on a postcard showing a fused image of Johnny Depp as Edward Scissorhands and a character with red hair and green winged eyebrows called Poison Ivy. He peeled off the post-it-note with Eve's flight information. On the back, she had written: "Just so you know, I'm on the continuum; it's Uma Thurman as much as Johnny Depp."

Morgan put the postcard in his bedside drawer along with the other trophies. He called Eve, despite it being late, and she sounded faraway as she joked about Johnny and Uma and admired their great cheekbones. She was on the green love seat drinking wine; Luke was away.

"I've booked a hotel," he told her. "But don't get too excited. I didn't shoot for the moon."

"We wouldn't want that," Eve mocked.

"And you know I won't be able to spend the whole time with you, right?"

"But I'd be such a hit at the anniversary dinner."

"Will Luke ask questions?"

"We're not like that," she said, and he winced at the intimate pronoun.

"I miss the taste of you."

"How do I taste?"

"Like moss, or fern, or maybe ..."

And then the phone went dead. Utterly dead. He tried calling back in five minutes and then ten. He checked his email. Then he lay in bed and wondered if Luke had come home unexpectedly.

At four in the morning, his phone buzzed a message. Eve had forgotten to charge her battery. She begged forgiveness; Morgan tried hard to swallow his rage.

He was late for work, but Zoe was off-site meeting advertisers and the office had a holiday air. Laptops stayed closed, phone calls meandered towards the personal, and coffee breaks stretched long. In this relaxed atmosphere, Morgan called Savannah.

She agreed, in principle, to the Q and A but pushed back on timings for the interview. If they moved it from November to December, he could shadow her for a week. In return, he could stay on at her place over the Christmas period and look after her dog.

There was no point telling her that journalists were not up for barter. By the time Zoe returned, Morgan had a proposal on her desk. To make the longer stay in Taos palatable, he'd suggested a Christmas feature that looked at different traditions: Indigenous Americans; the Muse in her lair; hippies who flocked to Taos in the sixties; Hispanic peoples; Catholics of all stripes. He was going to add capitalists as a joke, but Zoe might take it seriously. She read the single typed sheet in under a minute.

"Anything longer than a week is unpaid leave," she told him. "We'll cover accommodation, food and gas. If the subject puts you up for free, keep the difference. Don't tell anyone I said that."

"I'll take it to the grave; we don't want anyone thinking you're soft. I've got a road-trip angle too."

"Good. I want my pound of flesh."

His reply to Savannah was more cautious. He would do the interview in December, but he couldn't commit to more than a couple of days over Christmas. In truth, he saw himself riding out New Year under her eclectic roof. Eve had already told him Christmas was a big deal in her family, and that included Luke-shaped obligations. He was glad to get his plans in first.

She had sent three texts over the course of the day. The first had been an enquiry as to whether he'd received her apology. The second suggested they pick up where they left off. The third was merely a question mark.

Morgan ignored the first two messages, but he sent a

quick reply to the last. He was busy, he told her, but they could catch up over the next few days. But a few days came and went, and although he called Eve several times, she never picked up. On the morning of the fifth day, he sent a text asking if she was okay. Her reply was a rhetorical question: *It doesn't feel good to be ignored, does it?*

As August crawled into view, Morgan felt his anxiety rising as predictably as his mother's bread. On the day of his flight, rain clouds massed on the horizon and he imagined delays or worse. It wasn't until his plane taxied slowly across the slick runway at Madison airport that he allowed himself hope. Around him, most of the travelers ignored signs and wrenched their bags from overhead bins as if they were on a time trial. For once, Morgan breathed deeply and waited until half the passengers had gone before getting up from his seat.

A decade had passed since university days, but as he drove his rental though the east side of town things seemed much the same. Sofas slouched on sidewalks and porches staged impromptu parties evident from beer cans rattling around in gutters. He cut across the town's central artery and into the side veins where venture capitalists had funded university dreams. His own department had been housed in an ageing building crammed with disciplines of the less lucrative kind. The only saving grace had been a lake-side view and proximity to the students' union.

He drove on, past the in-town dairy, the Victorian homes built for faculty, and the superstores that kept a general populous entertained. It was late afternoon, and the lanes were doused in shadow. He had lost the battle and would stay one night at the farm.

"I don't ask much," had been Margaret's winning line. "I want you all together under one roof."

As the rental car juddered on down a winding lane, Morgan slowed to a crawl. One more turn, and he would glimpse the battered mailbox on the edge of his parents' property, a mailbox that had survived storms and occasional car crashes. But as he drew near, the first thing he noticed was the mailbox wasn't alone. A sign had sprung up since his last visit.

He passed the sign and began to turn into the driveway, but then he slammed the brakes and reversed at an angle to read three incomprehensible words. The first two, black and solid, shocked him; the third, a screaming red diagonal, chilled him to the bone: SOLD.

Morgan took his foot off the pedal and the car stalled. When he re-engaged the engine, he felt a childish urge to ram the sign into the ditch. Instead, he screeched down the entire length of his parent's drive, churning up gravel. He cut the engine, but he kept his lights on and stared up at the only place he had ever called home. Faith appeared, silhouetted against the bulk of the farm.

"You've seen the sign, I take it," she said, climbing into the passenger seat of his car. "It was a shock for me too. They have every right, of course, it's just…"

"We never thought it would happen."

"Exactly."

"Did Tom know?"

"He dealt with the sale."

"Of course, he did."

"Dinner's almost ready," Faith said. "They heard your graceful entrance; they'll be wondering where we are."

16

When Morgan opened the back door, he kicked it with such force paint flakes fluttered to the ground like snow. He sat on the bench his father had made one long ago summer and unlaced his boots. He'd helped with the bench, holding the spirit level and doing some sanding; it was one of a hundred memories he had of this house.

He stood and pushed through the swing doors that led into the kitchen where everyone was gathered. He caught his mother halfway between the stove and the table with a pan of roasted potatoes. She set the pan down and raised her oven gloves in a virtual embrace. Then, she told him to wash his hands.

"Quick," she chided," before the food gets cold."

He gave his hands a cursory rinse and approached the table where Jerry stood and Tom raised his whisky glass in mock salute. Morgan ignored them both and went straight to his father.

"I'm glad you're here, son," John said, patting Morgan's hand.

"I saw the sign, Dad. It was a shock. I would have liked some warning."

"Don't blame him," Margaret called, alert as ever. "I

asked him to keep quiet until it was all settled."

"But Tom knew, right?" Morgan asked.

"It wasn't personal," his brother said, in the careful tone he used for business settings.

"Not personal; no, it never is with you."

"Beer? Or something stronger?" Faith asked.

"Beer. Not ready for an old man's drink yet."

"I should check on the kids," Jerry said, with a nose for family tension.

Margaret had removed her apron and revealed a dress with bright yellow flowers. She looked as if she might block Jerry's path, but then she relented.

"Boys," she said, to her sons. "One of you carry the meat tray and the other one can carve."

Morgan claimed the tray, but he ignored her wishes and delivered the meat to his father like a prize.

"Very 1950's," commented Faith.

"What's 1950's?" asked Jerry, re-appearing with two plates and the remains of toast with jelly.

"Did they brush their teeth?" Faith asked, and Jerry looked stricken. "Oh well, the main thing is that they fall asleep. They fought in the car all the way here; Zach decapitated one of Bella's doll."

"Siblings can be cruel," Morgan observed.

During this exchange, his father had managed to carve only one slice of meat, and his hands shook visibly. It was too late for Morgan to fix his error; any attempt to wrest the meat away now would only make matters worse. Faith did her best and covered each tiny portion of meat with a mound of vegetables and streams of gravy.

Once they were all served, Margaret offered thanks and the room filled with the sounds of eating and desultory small talk. But all Morgan could focus on was the tremble of his father's hands and the fraught passage of food from fork to mouth.

"You thought you were being clever, didn't you?" Tom muttered, when he got up to refill his drink.

Dessert came courtesy of Jerry who produced two apple pies but forgot to warm them. Faith came to the rescue, and when Jerry apologized, she said he was a saint compared to other men. Margaret tapped her glass.

"It's good to have you all home," she said, "but it's late. We can talk business tomorrow. Morgan, you're in your old room. You'll find some boxes there. Please sort through them. The rest of you, sleep well."

With that, Margaret guided her husband out of the room with the help of their eldest son.

"When did they get so old?" Morgan asked Faith.

"You haven't been home in a while. The decline has been gradual. There goes Tom," she added, as they heard a car engine. "He probably shouldn't be driving."

"How come he gets to stay in a hotel and I have to be here for the night?"

"Maybe those boxes?" Faith surmised. "You know how our mother likes us to purge our childhood possessions."

They laughed and compared stories of motherly disdain. But then Morgan grew serious again and asked why Faith had been so quick to defend their brother.

"Because I'm in the middle and see both sides," she said, hugging him, a short, tight squeeze before they left the kitchen for the cold interior of the farm.

When morning arrived in a sweat of suffocation, Morgan beat down the quilt that had ridden up over his head like a shroud. He surfaced to a world of green shag carpet and wood panel; startled, he lurched up and hit his head on the sloped ceiling where he'd once taped pictures of childhood heroes.

Across the room, three cardboard boxes awaited his attention. He padded over and examined the nearest one. There were action figures with missing limbs, a deflated football, the dried-up baseball mitt he'd inherited from Tom. The second box held text books, a set of dominoes, a wonky compass and a few baseball cards. It was the third box that produced any real treasure. Down at the bottom, underneath an old football jersey, he found a composition book with a photograph of Sideways taped on the cover.

He got back into bed and flipped through the pages. It was a diary, written in his spidery hand with short entries focused on single events such as an incident at school, an act of treachery by Tom, a trick that Sideways had mastered alongside oddly proportioned drawings of his dog. On the very last page, he'd written a poem titled: 'True Friend'. He read it aloud now, smiling at the words that sloped together in a rush of affection.

He dressed and went down to the kitchen, where he found his sister sipping coffee by the back door.

"It's a good thing Tom never saw that," she said, when Morgan showed her the poem. "He'd have teased the stuffing out of you."

"I can't believe Mom didn't throw this away; she always hated my dog."

"Hated? No, she felt upstaged. Do you want breakfast? Dad is already in his shed, and Mom is doing a load of laundry. No sign of Tom."

"I'll grab some toast," he said. "But first, I'm going out to see our father."

He went around the house and along the worn path to his father's shed where he knocked and entered without waiting for a reply. John was hunched over a disassembled radio. The building was damp and the windows clouded; it was smaller than Morgan remembered and not as clean.

"What are you working on?" he asked, although it was obvious.

"I told Margaret I'd mend this radio, but I'm darned if I can figure out what's wrong."

When the tremor of his father's hands grew too pronounced, Morgan went to the rear of the shed where garden implements hung straight and clean.

"Couldn't we get her a new radio?" he asked.

"You don't throw things away, son, just because they're old. Anyway, it wouldn't be the same."

Morgan thought of the boxes in his room, most of the contents destined for the trash, and returned to his father's workbench. He picked up a piece of the casing, trying to picture where the radio had sat in the house. The kitchen, he thought, so Margaret could listen to news.

"About selling the farm, Dad..."

"Your mother's idea. We're moving to Florida."

"Florida?" he exclaimed, dropping the casing and causing his father to make an impatient noise in the back of his throat. "I'm sorry, but I've never heard you mention Florida before."

They both stooped to retrieve the casing, but Morgan got there first.

"It's a done deal," John said, gripping his screwdriver more tightly. "It's what your mother wants. We've made good money on this place; there'll be some left over for you three after we're settled."

"I've never cared about that. You love the farm. What will happen to your shed?"

"I've told Chuck he can have it, as long as he moves it lock, stock and barrel. His wife will kill him, but he'll do it anyway. He's got that field behind his house."

"Are you sure you'll be happy in Florida?"

"Why not? It's a place like any other. Now, if you don't mind, I need to finish this job."

It was the same polite dismissal that Morgan remembered from childhood. There was no point resisting. He left the shed but leaned back against the door and heard a splash of music followed by quiet. For one sweet moment, his father had got the radio working.

He was halfway to the house when Zach burst from the woods shaped like a spear and dived at his uncle's legs. Morgan sidestepped, with all the native skill of a younger brother, and held his nephew away with a hand on the boy's head.

"You'll need to bulk up if you want to take me down," he laughed, as Jerry puffed into view.

Morgan released Zach, but only so he could tap Jerry's stomach and quiz him about pie consumption.

"It's not pie," Jerry complained. "I have steak coming out of every orifice. Eating out comes with the job."

They walked back to the house, and Morgan promised his nephew he would sit next to him at the anniversary dinner.

"I have to wear a suit and everything," Zach complained.

"I know, buddy, but you'll look sharp."

Sharper than his uncle, at least. Morgan had bought a new shirt for the occasion, but he'd wear it with wrinkled chinos and an ancient jacket. He might have to borrow a tie from Jerry.

"Why are you up this early anyway?" he asked his brother-in-law. "Are you still in the dog house?"

"Your sister gave me a long list of tasks for tonight's anniversary dinner, and it's not that early."

Morgan glanced at his watch. It was the first time he had thought of Eve since he had arrived home. She must be wondering what had become of him.

17

Morgan arrived at the hotel, and the receptionist told him that Ms Thurman was across the street at the Lazy Spoon Café."

"I couldn't resist," Eve laughed, when he found her there. "But the receptionist was so young, I don't think she's even heard of Uma."

"I can't believe you're actually here."

"I'm here, but feeling a little neglected."

"Let me remedy that," he said. "I'll get a coffee to go and then you can show me our room."

Back at the hotel, the receptionist seemed glad to have brought them together. Morgan wished he had been bold enough to register as Mr. Depp.

"Welcome to our boudoir," Eve said, opening the door to room 272.

It was filled, already, with Eve's graceful touches: a bowl of fruit in the kitchen area, books on one of the side tables, flowers and the now familiar café press. He closed the door, threw down his bag and pulled Eve close.

"So urgent," she whispered.

Their teeth clashed and Eve's mouth tasted sour from coffee. She pushed him away.

"Remember what we promised," she said. "We have to be good. I already feel as if I'm stealing moments from other people."

He left his bags near the door, and they drove downtown to eat African stew in the basement of a former bank. They gazed at each other as they tore fermented bread into pieces to scoop their food and let the juices run through their fingers. Sated, they walked hand-in-hand without caution under a cloud-filled sky.

When a cold wind blew in from the lake, they took refuge in a fair-trade store that was filled with the earth's plunder. Eve asked to look at rings, and the young woman with sharp cheekbones and heavy dreadlocks produced two velvet trays laden with silver bands. Eve chose a Celtic design and then asked if there were rings for men. Dreadlocks dipped down again and brought up a tray with heavier bands.

Morgan tried to focus on the rings, but his attention was drawn to the duck-egg pendant hanging around the woman's neck; it was so heavy it made her tendons bulge. Eve chose for him in the end, a leaping stag design. He wanted to say that he hated rings and found them confining, but he stayed mute because Eve seemed happy.

Out on the street, rings already on their fingers, they walked in a buffeting wind. Eve said she wanted to go back to the hotel and watch a movie, and it was only when they got back to their room that he noticed they had twin beds instead of a queen.

"I'm going to complain," he said. "They screwed up the booking."

"Don't. It was me who made the change."

"Why?"

"You know why," she said. "Come; we can still lie here on one of the beds and watch a film together."

As Eve flipped through the channels, Morgan fidgeted and thumped pillows. When she chose a black-and-white movie about a group of nuns trying to convert local heathens out in the wild west, he crossed his arms and dozed. He woke just as a youngest nun had earned the respect of the leather-faced hero.

"What happened?" he asked.

"She fell in love with the cowboy, but she gave him up in the name of religious duty."

"Did they at least make out?"

"They shared one passionate kiss, but then she remembered her calling."

"Too bad," he said. "Not my choice of an ending."

He levered himself up on one elbow and brushed a strand of hair from Eve's face; he thought she might have been crying. She ducked away from him and got up to close the curtains. She seemed restless and complained that the hour before dusk filled her with dread. She needed to be among crowds.

Morgan chose an Irish pub near the Capitol where the barman greeted them with a burst of song and kissed Eve's hand. They ordered beers and sat on tall stools, sharing roasted peanuts out of a wooden bowl.

"Quite the performance," Morgan commented.

"Oscar worthy," Eve agreed. "You can leave me here with a clear conscience. I can get a cab back to the hotel."

He didn't want to leave her at all, but he was due back at the farm; he paid for the beers and left a twenty to cover any tab. He resisted an urge to punch the man when he told Morgan he would keep a very close eye on Eve.

"Where have you been?" Faith asked. "Mom's already gone to check on the band. She's afraid they'll be too young to know any of her tunes."

"If she's in a mood, I need one of Jerry's ties."

When Faith gave him a purple monstrosity, Morgan protested. But she assured him it would distract from the black shoes that so obviously clashed with his jacket. He'd be lucky to make it through the night without causing offence.

Landings Supper Club was spruced up for the occasion too, with white tablecloths, center-pieces of real flowers, and a huge banner that congratulated the happy couple. But not even moody red lanterns could hide the ceiling stains and the carpet had seen better days. Despite this, the mood was festive and the band, reassuringly ancient, in full swing when they arrived. He hoped they had quieter numbers for the meal; there were already demands to 'say that again' in almost every conversation.

When the evening hit peak nostalgia, Tom gave a syrupy speech about their parents' husbandry of the farm and their enduring union. He called on them to raise a glass to the couple who 'did it right' from the beginning. Morgan mimed applause then snuck out of the over-heated room in the glare of his sister's disapproving gaze. Jerry had taken the kids home, but Faith was stuck for the duration.

Outside, he bummed a cigarette from the young valet and reclaimed his keys. As he drove away, the supper club glowed like a spaceship threatening to lift off with the old people on board. Poor Faith; the best she could hope for was the ancients running out of gas.

Free and clear of family obligation, Morgan pulled over and called Eve. Her phone went straight to voicemail, and he wondered if she was flirting with the barman or back in their room. He stopped at the hotel, just in case, and the man-boy on duty said his wife was out by the pool. He found her reclined on a lounger and sipping red wine.

"Surprised?" she asked. "How did it go?"

"Slow torture," he admitted.

"Made worse by imagining me with Colm?"

"Was that his name? Irish, my ass."

She laughed and suggested they walk in the grassy area beyond the pool. There was a pond stocked with fish, she said, and they might see a pair of nesting herons.

"You're still wearing your ring," she commented. "I thought you might take it off for the party."

He didn't tell her he had tried, but his finger had swollen, and there had been no time to use soap.

"We could do a ritual with our rings," Eve said, as they stood near the edge of the pond, admiring the reflection of trees in the moon-lit water. "It could help us feel linked when we're apart."

He let her work the ring off his finger, looser now in the cool night air, and she held it in the palm of her hand and looked solemn.

"I will tell the truth and love you however I can," she said, sliding the ring back on his finger. "Your turn."

Morgan received Eve's ring, held it for a few self-conscious moments and then spoke: "I will do my best to live up to your expectations."

Eve gave him a sideways glance but said nothing. The evening wound down and they returned to their room and separate beds, only to be jerked awake some hours later by a piercing alarm.

"What the hell was that?" Morgan asked, as he struggled to sit upright.

"Must be a fire drill," Eve replied, closing the book she'd been reading. "It's not even 5:00 a.m."

She made no effort to dress; instead, she wrapped a bedspread around her upper body and waited as Morgan pulled on t-shirt and jeans. They joined the flow of disheveled guests grumbling their way to the exits.

In the parking lot, man-boy from reception spoke through a hand-held megaphone and told them they could go back to bed.

"Nothing on the barbecue tonight, folks," he added, which made Eve snort with laughter.

A man in boxer shorts said they should get some compensation for the distress.

"Free breakfast," man-boy promised with a broad smile.

"Our fellow guests are not exactly on the genius spectrum," Eve said, in an undertone.

They were too wired to sleep, so they spent the next hour gossiping about the boy with the pet Iguana and the woman struggling with a huge basket of cosmetics.

"What would you save in a fire?" Morgan asked.

"At home, it would be my letters and a picture or two."

He wondered if she meant love letters and if his own scribbles would make the grade. He told her, although she hadn't asked, that he would save the composition book he had just discovered which was also a love letter of sorts.

"But I was talking about human relationships," Eve said. "It's not quite the same."

He was about to argue, but Eve got up and went into the kitchen area to make coffee; she seemed to regard the conversation closed. He stretched out on his bed and exhaled loudly. Surely Eve, of all people, knew how significant Sideways had been; she had commended his writing at the retreat. He watched her settle into a chair and crack the spine of her book.

"The binding will unglue if you do that,' he said. "Books are precious you know."

"Okay, Morgan, I get it," Eve sighed, without looking up. "Your dog mattered to you."

She sipped her coffee and kept her head buried in her book, signaling again that there was nothing more to say. Unable to bear it any longer, Morgan said that he was going out to buy bagels; he knew a place that opened early seven-days-a-week. She made no effort to stop him, but gave a half-smile which seemed to say that it was no business of hers.

Morgan passed man-boy at reception, and the two of them exchanged a look which seemed to acknowledge that the day had begun badly for both of them.

Downtown, the streets were quiet; flags and streamers left over from Saturday's game drooped like weary party-goers. He parked and wandered through the student union and out to the lake where he played kickball with an old food carton. A duck eyed him with disdain and waddled off, bright purple patches glaring back amidst a uniform of drab feathers.

He found the bagel place from memory. A line stretched out the door, and he waited behind two young women who were underdressed for the season. They wore flip-flops but carried high heels in canvas bags and they seemed to have by-passed sleep entirely. He listened in on their conversation about cheating boyfriends and awkward one-night stands.

At the front of the line, he ordered coffee and bagel holes; he took them over to a table by the window and sat in full reporter mode watching the world go by and making notes on a napkin.

When he was finished, he bought a fresh bag of bagels with cream cheese and drove back to the hotel. But the room was empty, so he took a shower and made inroads on the bagels himself as he waited for Eve.

"Appetizing," she said, an hour later, eying the cold remains. "We should get out of here; we only have a half-day before I head home."

Just like that, Morgan regretted a morning that he now saw had been wasted on students and ducks.

18

They ended up in church. It was Eve who noticed the looming structure on the west side of town. The bells were ringing for morning service, so she made him park and then propelled him up the steps.

"This is the perfect thing," she said. "It will mend our tender hearts."

They wandered down the center aisle, and Morgan imagined the sound of their footsteps drifting up to God who must surely live in the rafters. It was strange, he thought, that the Lord chose to dwell in such stone-cold places.

He paused, along with Eve, in front of a plaster cast of Mary whose arms stretched out across a sea of candles that threatened to set her alight. Eve took a fresh candle and touched the wick to an already existing flame. The smell of wax was overpowering.

They sat in a pew halfway between the altar and freedom. Morgan left a respectful gap between them, but Eve slid close until their thighs touched. Then the organ surged into life, and a priest wearing elaborate robes swished past them followed by an older woman burdened with a cumbersome cross.

At the rear, a motley crew of choir members plodded forward and struggled to sing in Latin. Morgan schooled his features to neutral as the priest lowered his bulk onto an ornate throne.

It was the woman who led them in prayer, but her voice trembled as she sought footing in this mostly masculine world. Then the priest ascended to his pulpit and proceeded to kiss the book he clearly assumed was the Bible. But what if someone had slipped *Moby Dick* up there or *Great Expectations*? Would it really matter? He must ask Eve who always claimed there was no 'the church' in her way of thinking.

Morgan endured the whole tedious pantomime for the pleasure of touching Eve's leg. When it was over and they flew down the steps to freedom, Eve said she was hungry, so they found a Lebanese place with a tasting menu pasted in the window. They were short on time, but Eve wanted the full experience, and she drew him inside to sit at a low table with floor cushions that reminded him of the retreat. He worried aloud about her missing her flight again.

"What if we forget my flight and you drive me to Minneapolis instead."

It was a statement more than a question, and it was delivered in a tone that suggested Eve was conferring a favor. He told her it was impossible to drive there and back in time for his own flight, unless he got the red-eye.

"Would you do that?" Eve asked. "Would you do that for me?"

He pictured his mother's disappointed face and his father's mournful smile. They expected him back at the farm for the long-delayed family conversation. But he already knew their Florida news. What else was there to say? He could get the details later from Faith.

Out on the sidewalk, he wrangled over the phone with the airlines and returned victorious. But when he told Eve, she showed neither surprise nor pleasure.

"My parents will be disappointed," he said

"Don't do it if it feels wrong," she retorted. "I thought you wanted more time together."

"I do; of course, I do. Ignore me. It's done."

Hummus, pitta, baba ghanoush and dolma wrestled in his belly as Morgan drove the unrelenting miles north and then west. Once safely on the road, Eve had become animated. She told stories and popped Jolly Ranchers into both of their mouths. From time to time, she landed soft fingers on his knee or the back of his neck. It was only as they neared the outskirts of Minneapolis that her hands went to her lap and she became subdued.

"I think you can take me all the way home," she said. "Luke's out for the day. It's the grey house with the purple front door. Those are my ferns."

The plants grew in such delicate profusion the slender aspen in their midst appeared like a Guru in front of a sycophantic crowd. He wondered how they survived a winter.

"Is it okay to use your bathroom?" he asked. "Since Luke's away."

She hesitated and glanced towards the house, as if seeking permission; a wind chime did two somersaults on the lowest branch of the aspen.

"I could pee in a cup," Morgan offered, "but it could get messy."

She laughed and they approached the front door where she plucked a key from under a pot. Inside, he glimpsed an airy kitchen-dining room as well as the green love seat notorious from late night calls.

"The bathroom's down there," Eve said, pointing to a corridor lined with photographs that reminded him of his visit to Gill. One shot showed a young man in a felt hat who looked straight to camera; he knew, without being told, that it was Luke. A good-looking man, but there was something haunted about the eyes.

The bathroom was the size of any confessional and

painted dark green. Morgan was careful not to leave traces, although a part of him wished that he could. When he was finished, Eve was in the same spot he had left her, ready to escort him out.

"So, that's the famous green love seat," he said, looking over her shoulder.

"Yup."

"And it looks like you have a decent back yard. What's the building out there?"

"It's where I go to write or to be alone."

He asked to see it, and she led him out and around the side of the building across a tired lawn dotted with dandelions. A path led up to the hideaway, and someone had planted tiny purple flowers in the gaps between stones. But Eve said they were violets that seeded themselves.

"Does your hideaway have a name?" he asked.

"Not really. Luke calls it Eve's Eyrie, but I'm not wild about that name."

The building was grey, same as the main house, but the roof was pitched high and made of tin. In the eaves, a porthole window caught the sun's glare.

"When it rains, the sound is immense," she said.

"It would drive me crazy," Morgan admitted.

The front entrance was made from reclaimed wood and had an old bean hook for a handle. Eve made a show of trying the door, but it was locked; she said the key was not to hand. He peered in through a window and commented on the narrow single bed against one wall.

"That's the point," Eve said. "Space for one."

He turned his face sideways against the glass and saw a small desk with a notepad and pen. Above the desk, a single vase sat on a simple wooden shelf.

"Minimalist," he commented. "What's on the card propped against that vase?"

But Eve had moved away, and he followed her along the garden fence. She told him that Luke had done all the work except for the electricals.

"Pity the window looks onto the neighbor's fence."

"I like it just as it is," Eve replied.

He knew better than to linger. He told her he was glad he knew where she lived and would picture her writing in the eyrie. He wanted to ask if the trip to Madison had been worth it and if she regretted their twin beds. Instead, he let her thank him for driving her home.

Hours later, when he was hit with late fees as well as a refueling charge, he thought he had paid too high a price on many levels. And when he turned his phone back on, silenced for church, there were multiple voicemails from Faith as well a text in all-caps. It was too late to call now, and it would be too early when he reached Seattle.

He slept most of the flight and went straight to the office after he landed. No one was there, and he dozed gently amid the hum of computers. At seven, he made coffee and called Faith.

"Thanks for having my back," he said.

"How do you know I did?"

"I just know."

"Why didn't you call? Mom was worried."

He apologized and made up a story about a friend who had needed him.

"What friend? she asked, suspiciously. "And why did he need *you?*"

He ignored the implied insult and said the friend's name was Luke, and he'd just found out his wife couldn't conceive. He had no idea why he'd used that name or why he made up the lie. But it worked and Faith de-escalated.

"I'll call Mom," he promised. "Did you find out what's happening to the old place?"

"Brace yourself," she warned. "It's going to be turned into a luxury golf course."

"You're kidding me. That's Tom all over."

"To be fair, he got them a lot of money, and it's not like any of us wanted to live there."

When he rang his mother, Morgan pictured bulldozers turning the farm to dust and rubble. Only his father's shed would escape as long as Chuck kept his word.

"I hear it's going to be a golf course," he began, but Margaret cut him off.

He had ruined the weekend and upset his father. Why couldn't he be more like Tom? Why indeed? He told her he was sorry and accepted the stigma of unreliable son. What he did not do was repeat the lie he had told Faith.

"Should I be worried about you?" Zoe asked, days later. "I've never seen you this focused on work."

"Isn't that a good thing?" Morgan challenged.

"Yes, except you seem joyless. I almost miss the lazier version."

"If it makes you feel better, I need some more time off to help my parents move."

But when he called his mother to confirm he would help in whatever way was needed, she was unimpressed.

"You were just here," she said. "Not that we really saw you. I suppose you could clear the attic. But don't expect me to wait on you hand and foot, I'm far too busy."

When he arrived at the farm the following Friday, it was bathed in autumn light and his mother had just gathered in the laundry. She thrust garbage bags into his hands and said she would be up soon to give more instructions. He noticed a tear in her stocking near the left ankle; by tomorrow, it would be gone.

Upstairs, his room was just as he had left it; no one had even made the bed. He dumped his overnight bag and went along the landing to open the attic hatch. The last time he'd been up there was decades before during a game of hide-and-seek. He'd managed to outlast Faith, but only because she abandoned the game without him knowing.

As he climbed the ladder now, Morgan kept his breath shallow to avoid breathing in dust. There were footprints on the weathered boards where someone had dragged boxes into three distinct groups. He opened the first box just as his mother's voice floated up from below.

"The pile on the left is for the dump. Clothes and toys are for the Salvation Army and need to go in bags. Anything in boxes gets stored in the barn."

He followed her commands exactly, relieved by the narrowness of his task. When he'd stacked the last box in what passed for a barn, Margaret ordered him to get his father from the shed.

"Let him know there's banana bread," she said. "I made it fresh this morning."

"My favorite; I might almost think I'd been forgiven."

"Who says I made it for you?" she asked, but she gave a slight smile which vanished when Morgan returned with the news that John was not hungry.

"That man," she said. "He's so stubborn. There'll be no shed in Florida. What will he do?"

They sat together, mother and son, and ate banana bread at the kitchen table. When conversation dried up, Morgan observed that his father had finally given up trying to make an English lawn.

"He has not given up," Margaret cried, slamming the table so hard she dislodged the butter dish. "It's not his fault he couldn't keep things going."

"I didn't mean it as criticism," Morgan apologized, bending down to pick up the broken butter dish. "Is he struggling? Why didn't you say? I could have…"

"Could have what? You have your own life. For heaven's sake, leave that; I'll deal with it later."

She put her head in her hands, and he had never seen her so defeated. He came around the table and knelt beside her, daring to hold her hand.

"What's really going on?" he asked. "I've noticed Dad's tremors; they seem to be getting worse."

Margaret gave him a long hard stare, as if gauging his

capacity for difficult truths. Then she told him that something was pressing on his father's brain. He hadn't wanted any of them to know.

"But Tom knows, right? And he thinks Florida is where old people go to live out their days playing golf and eating ice cream."

Margaret smiled then grew somber again and talked about the brain specialist in Florida who was the best in his field.

"But it's so far away," he protested.

"We won't be alone. Tom got a place there."

"Tom in Florida? I can't picture that."

"He's tired of New York; it's a fresh start. You know, your father would have hated to live in a nearby retirement home knowing the farm had gone."

"Well, that's true," Morgan admitted.

"You should be grateful to your brother. Tom paid the down-payment on that apartment of yours."

"You said it was a nest egg you had saved."

"He asked us to say that; he thought you might not accept the money if you knew. Enough talk; you get on with clearing that attic."

Morgan brought down the rest of the discards and got to work loading the farm truck for the dump. He did it haphazardly, disturbed by the conversation with his mother, not bothering to rope anything down. His mind was full of the news about his father and Tom. It seemed to him that the usual family hierarchies were in disarray.

19

The dump was further out than Morgan remembered, and the truck shook and rattled the whole way there. He unloaded the scrap books, lamps that hadn't worked in years, saucepans without lids and bits of wood from various carpentry projects. After he'd pushed the last items off with his feet, he swept the flat-bed out with an old broom. Gulls swooped in and wheeled away, disgusted by the meagre pickings.

He was about to get back in the truck when his phone rang. In the background, he heard doors banging, laughter and then Eve's familiar voice on the line.

"I need to see you," she said.

"Is everything okay? Where are you?"

"I'm using the pay phone in a bar. If I fly out next weekend, can we go somewhere?"

"We could take a trip out to the Peninsula," he said, trying to keep the excitement out of his voice. "We could hike on the mainland and then ferry out to an island for the night. Or two nights?"

"You decide," she told him. "Whatever you think. I'll call you with flight details."

She hung up quickly, and he wondered if she'd been

drinking and would come to regret the call. He would book a place but not count on her coming. But if she did come, he would tell her about Margaret's revelations. Eve might have insights about his father's condition and care. It would be good to talk to someone outside the family.

Back at the farm, there was no sign of Margaret, but John was in the living room by an unlit fire.

"Shall I get that going?" Morgan asked.

"Not cold enough," his father replied.

"Does it have to be freezing before you allow yourself some comfort? You need to take better care."

"I'm fine; Margaret takes excellent care of me."

"Where is she anyway?" Morgan asked.

"She's checking the boxes you stacked."

They both laughed, and John offered to keep Morgan company on his next run to the dump. It had been ages since he'd been out there.

"You will not," his wife said, appearing by magic. "The dump is the last place you belong."

Morgan thought about her choice of words the next morning, as he loaded the truck for a second run. He was going early in an effort to avoid church, but he needn't have worried. When he got back to the farm, his parents were still not dressed.

"Your father had a bad night," Margaret explained. "Do you still want to help?"

"Of course; anything you need."

"I just got word the specialist had a cancellation. I can meet with him on Tuesday."

"You want me to go with you?" he guessed.

"Of course not. Tom's coming. I want you to stay here and make your father eat and take his pills.

"How long will you be gone?"

"Four days at most. There are casseroles in the freezer, so you won't have to do much. But if you think it's beyond you, I can always ask Faith."

"I can do it," he said, ignorant of the fact that his mother had already asked his sister who'd been much too busy to come.

"Don't take it personally," Faith advised, when they spoke on the phone later. "You know Mom is old-fashioned. She thinks Dad needs a woman in the house. What's up with you anyway? You sound down."

"I've spent the weekend running between a dusty attic and a landfill, all while being massively under-appreciated by our mother."

"Poor you! And now you have to play nurse; let's hope Dad survives."

It seemed to Morgan that he occupied the lowest rung of the family ladder. He recovered slightly when Margaret asked if they would miss him at work, but then she called it a newspaper instead of a magazine. At least his father was pleased; they would rub along well, he told Morgan, as long as he wasn't expected to cook. Margaret hadn't let him near the kitchen in years.

"Haven't let you?" Margaret snorted. "You don't even know how to boil an egg. At least in Florida, I won't have to do all your cooking."

"Is that true?" Morgan asked.

"Hot food available all day long," John confirmed. "Part of the package. It's a retirement home you see."

"He exaggerating; it's assisted-living."

"If that's what you both want, then I'm happy for you," Morgan said.

"What a relief to get my son's blessing," Margaret shot back.

In the early morning, the low growl of the water heater told him that Margaret was awake. There was no shower in his parents' bathroom, just a hose contraption you fixed to the taps that worked as long as you didn't mind leaks and temperature surges. Morgan knelt up in bed and peered out through the curtains.

The clouds were low, and snow was forecast; he hoped Margaret would make it out in time. He waited fifteen minutes then dressed and went down to the kitchen where his mother was making porridge. As soon as she saw him, she fired off a list of last-minute instructions. If it snowed, his father should stay indoors and not do any shoveling. If Morgan didn't know how something worked, he should call Faith. She'd put casseroles in the freezer along with mixed vegetables and a few pies.

"Basically, food to last until Armageddon."

"Your father's upstairs," she said, ignoring him. "This is his porridge. We've already said our goodbyes. I'll be back in a few days. You'll be fine."

"Are you trying to convince me or yourself?" Morgan asked, helping her on with her coat.

He watched her do up the buttons with fingers that were steady but curved like wishbones and carried her bag out to the waiting cab. The sight of her, head erect and motionless through the cab's back window, made him wish he had said something kind. His mother was brave. What did she know about brain tumors, medical specialists, or even Florida come to that?

The first snowflakes arrived late that morning but didn't stick around. By the time John appeared in the kitchen, Morgan had eaten his father's porridge and drunk three mugs of coffee. They agreed it was too cold for the shed, and his father said that in any case he didn't want to risk a fall on Morgan's watch.

"I'll sit in the living room," he offered. "The snow's pretty; there won't be any of that where we're going."

When Morgan looked in on him, John had fallen asleep in a chair. He lit the fire and scoured websites for places to stay with Eve. The Peninsula quivered with holiday lets, but last-minute bookings were hard to find. He lucked out with a bed and breakfast that had a late cancellation. It boasted apple orchards, water views, and late check-out.

He booked two nights and sent Eve a message. Instead of catching the ferry from Seattle, they could meet at the airport and drive down in one car. If they got there by late afternoon, they could hike an old-growth forest in the National Park then ferry over to the island for dinner.

When his father woke mid-afternoon, he still wasn't hungry. Mindful of Margaret's instructions, Morgan made a plate of cheese-and-pickle sandwiches for them to share. He also quartered an apple and left the peel intact. They played scrabble and didn't bother with napkins, both of them dropping crumbs on the board. Margaret would have hated such carelessness, but without her supervision they were free to do as they pleased.

At dusk, a fawn stumbled past the window in search of food. Blizzard conditions had been predicted overnight and as much as thirteen inches of snow. Morgan thought about cutting maple branches, but if the fawn was an orphan it would have to learn how to forage for itself. He attended to human needs instead; he filled the log baskets and secured a tarp over the extra wood.

"Lucky your mother got out when she did," his father said. "If you don't mind, I might have an early night. We can save the casserole for tomorrow."

Morgan listened for his father's footsteps overhead, and when the bedroom door clicked shut, got a whiskey bottle from the liquor cabinet under the stairs. He half-filled a glass and settled by the now-blazing fire.

Back when they were teens, he and Tom had used the age-old trick of stealing liquor and adding water to cover the theft. Even though their father must have noticed the dilution, he never once ratted them out. He wished the old man hadn't gone to bed so soon.

When Morgan woke, sun had crept into the yard; the snow had stopped falling, but wind had arrived to play sculptor. Tree trunks were stippled white, and huge drifts has risen against the side of the house in waves.

Morgan threw on a coat and work boots and pushed open the resistant back door. His mouth felt like cardboard, and his body had been contorted into strange shapes by the ancient sofa cushions. He did jumping-jacks in the doorway and stepped outside only to sink to his knees in fresh snow. It took him five minutes to make a circumference of the house.

With sweat gathering under layers, Morgan grabbed a shovel and began to clear the walkways. Near the shed, an opossum poked his nose from behind the back-up log-store. The creature's hair was wet and parted in the middle old-man style; he scrambled onto the deck and over flower pots to reach the bird seed container which he attempted to open with his pink, hairless toes.

The animal's comic maneuvers made Morgan smile; he flung down his shovel and begin to roll snow into two large balls. Once the body and the head of the snowman were complete, he broke off twigs for the arms and found pine cones to make a face.

The finished product was lopsided - quite different from the ones he had made in the past with Tom. He was still admiring his handiwork when a text buzzed in from Eve. She would drive alone to the Peninsula alone and meet him there.

He returned the phone to his pocket and eyed the snowman. Then, he did what he had wanted to do so often back in his childhood years. He took careful aim and kicked the snowman square in the belly so that the head went flying.

"That didn't last long," his father called, from the back door.

"Dad. You'll catch your death. It's too cold to be out here in pajamas. I'll make us some coffee. Go and put on something warm."

Later, when they sat at the kitchen table, his father asked why he had destroyed the snowman. Morgan told him he was laying old resentments to rest.

"Remember how Tom was so particular? He used to make me measure the ratio of head to body on every snowman we ever made. He took all of the fun out of playing."

"He would have made a fine engineer," his father said, wistfully. "If he hadn't missed so much school, he might have done engineering instead of business studies."

"I don't remember him missing school."

"You were too young. When Margaret went away, Tom had to be responsible. Are the bird feeders empty? I can't tell with all this snow."

"It's on my list," Morgan assured him.

"Do it now," his father said.

As Morgan brushed snow from the feeders, he wondered if his father was confused. Nowhere in his memory was a time when it was just four of them without his mother. He'd ask Faith, or, worse case scenario, Tom.

20

At noon, a man arrived with a snow plough and cleared the long drive. He waved an arm in Morgan's direction but didn't stay to receive thanks. Country folk were like that, he thought, short on word but long on deed. In the city, he barely knew his neighbors.

They ate the first of Margaret's casseroles at lunch and talked about the weather. In the afternoon, they played Scrabble again until John floundered over one-syllable words. After that, they each read sections of the local paper, commenting back and forth until it was time for tea, a tradition they kept in homage to their English ancestors.

As they drank the milky substance and munched on Margaret's cookies, they argued over whether the fawn was still alive. His father claimed the coyotes would have got him, but Morgan imagined him safe on higher ground. By day's end they had made a small wager, but when Morgan found the carcass, picked almost clean, he covered it with snow and told no one.

When Margaret returned, along with the thaw, she arrived in the same cab as the one that had carried her away. She appeared pale yet resolute as she marched into her kitchen and began to listen to Morgan's account of the preceding days with sharp nods of her head. It felt strange talking about his father, as if he and his mother had colluded in the care of a willful child.

When he asked how it had gone with the specialist, she said she liked him well enough and he had answered all of her questions. She had also viewed the apartment which was smaller than she hoped. With this sparse report concluded, she went upstairs to check on her husband.

In the end, no one thanked him. Margaret propelled him over her threshold with a push of her bony hands. It was icy, despite the thaw, and Morgan walked with care around the side of the house. Without permission, he took one of the bird feeders and carried it back to his car.

His drive to the airport was slow, balletic, since the rental struggled to find traction. He wondered if he had seen the farm for the last time. If so, it hadn't been the worst kind of ending. Time with his father had been companionable, and the episode with the snowman had felt just right. He put on headphones for the flight home and listened to the Red Hot Chili Peppers most of the way to Seattle.

Only when he landed did Morgan allow himself to think about Eve and her choice to drive alone to the Peninsula. There must be a logical explanation, he thought, and the most important thing was having two days and nights together. He hoped she had missed him.

United with his truck, Morgan drove with the radio on and the windows down. It was a warm fall day and the trees around Olympia had started to turn. When he arrived at the gateway to Olympic National Park, he felt a rush of optimism. He parked on a rough patch of ground and walked towards the wooden pier that seemed to be the main feature of this one-track town.

A solitary fisherman was bent over a line. Morgan asked if he'd had any bites, and the man smiled and lifted his rod out of the water. He had an utterly bare line.

"Gets me out of the house," he said, with a phlegmy

chuckle. "I keep telling the herons I don't have a lure, so I can't catch fish; they don't seem to believe me."

On cue, a heron landed and took off again with its peculiar ungainly flight and the man began to pack up his gear. Morgan wondered why he didn't just fish for real, but he didn't feel he could ask.

The town was also in its final act of the day. Hands pulled shutters closed and displays vanished into interiors. Only the diner, tucked between a guesthouse and a liquor store, flashed an open sign. He went in, ordered coffee and checked his phone; but there was no message from Eve, although her flight would have landed hours before.

When he'd been in the diner for a while, Morgan called Eve's phone, but it went straight to voicemail. He waited fifteen minutes and called again; this time, he left a message and tried to keep his voice light. By the time he'd recorded his third message, his anxiety was palpable and he walked back up main street towards his truck.

It was quiet on the road. Occasional headlights loomed and vanished, but none of these vehicles brought Eve. He thought of driving back the way he had come but instead moved his truck closer to the diner. Back inside, the waitress poured a fresh mug of coffee without being asked and gave him a slice of pie.

It was hard not to imagine an accident of some kind. If so, would anyone know where Eve was? Would he be called upon to explain their mutual presence on the Peninsula? He went outside again, but before he could leave a fourth message, Eve came walking down the road with her phone up to her ear

"No service," she said. "I'm just getting your messages now. So many messages."

"I thought something had happened to you," he said, fear turning to laughter.

"There was an accident; traffic got backed up."

It was too late to walk in the forest now, but Eve said

they should go there anyway and admire the trees. He insisted they travel in one vehicle, and he drove with his hand on her knee for as long as he could. The lights on his truck made cinema out of the dark pines, but a mile in, the road was blocked by an official park barrier. Morgan got out and read the notice, batting away insects from the truck's full beam.

"A fire," he said, when he returned to Eve. "Two months ago, but the park is closed for safety reasons."

"Do you think we could just ignore the sign?"

"Probably not. I'm guessing it's still unsafe."

The drive back to town felt anti-climactic. Eve got into her rental car and they caught the last ferry out to the island. He called the bed and breakfast and said they'd be having dinner first; their host promised to leave the door unlocked and said she would see them tomorrow.

The restaurant he'd chosen was casual yet intimate. The only other diners were an elderly couple and a woman eating alone with a book propped against a pepper grinder. Eve ordered a nut roast with seasonal veg while Morgan opted for chicken and mash along with a beer.

"Anything to drink for you, ma'am?" the young waiter asked Eve.

"Not ma'am," she laughed. "Never ma'am. I'll take a glass of house red."

"Excellent choice," he told her. "It's a Merlot with hints of berry and leather."

"Good eye contact," Eve commented, after the waiter had left them, "and a winning manner. He'll go far."

Not far enough, thought Morgan, when the boy returned almost immediately with a bottle of beer and Eve's wine which he placed before her like a glass slipper.

"You have to admit he's good," Eve laughed. "He even noticed I'm left-handed."

Conversation stayed on safe topics as they waited for their food. They discussed Eve's work, books on the New

York Times bestseller list, Jess's plan for a writing reunion early next year. When he asked about their joint writing project, Eve grew defensive but admitted they had barely got a concept and were arguing over the title.

Their food arrived and the waiter, unasked, brought Eve a second glass of wine from a vineyard that had escaped recent fires. It was a limited edition, he told her, but the bottle had been open two days and he didn't want it to go to waste. The wine mellowed Eve, and when the waiter came back to check on them, she said the nut roast was the best she'd ever tasted. Morgan let himself relax and ordered a second beer.

When Eve had finished eating, she pushed her plate away and leaned towards him across the table. There was something she needed to tell him, a recent development on the home front. He searched her face for clues. For one brief moment, he wondered if it was possible that Eve was about to leave her husband.

"Promise you won't be angry?" she asked, and his heart sank.

"How can I promise when I don't know what you're going to say?"

"Luke knows; he knows about us."

Hands appeared between them, and the waiter asked if they wanted dessert. There were two choices: a brownie or apple pie with whipped cream.

"Apple pie," Eve whispered.

"Two forks, cream on the side," Morgan added.

The pie came and they cut into it from both sides as Morgan asked for details; she told him that Luke had found some of her letters.

"You mean my letters?" he spluttered, spraying her with crumbs. "Jesus Christ. How the hell did that happen?"

"Don't. I've had enough of that from Luke."

"But how did he find them? Did he go through your things? Was he suspicious?"

"No, no. Nothing like that. It was my fault. I was re-reading them, and I must have left one out."

"Jesus Christ," he said, again, to the air.

He pictured Luke, a man he knew from a photograph, reading his letters with those sad, deep eyes. He knew he should feel remorse, empathy even, but all he experienced was cold, hard rage. Luke had no right to any of those letters.

"We had a terrible argument," Eve confessed. "It was dreadful. I agreed to do therapy. We need to see what's left of our marriage. I owe him that much."

"Therapy," Morgan repeated.

"Yes, therapy. It means that we can't see each other for a while, or talk, or anything."

She raised a forkful of pie and then set it down.

"That's it?" Morgan asked. "I'm just tossed aside like I don't even matter?"

"You do matter, but I'm married."

"Have you only just noticed?"

"Don't be sarcastic," Eve begged. "I never intended for this to happen. I'm sorry. We need to release each other…for now. I'm trying to be honest with everyone."

"Bit late for that. Does Luke even know that you're here?"

"He thinks I'm with Jess," she admitted. "And I will be soon."

"Hah! So not on board with the honesty just yet."

He raised a hand and called for the check. The waiter appeared, as if he'd been hovering nearby. He put a piece of paper in front of Morgan but asked Eve if she was okay. She nodded and gave a smile of reassurance.

"And there goes your tip, buddy," muttered Morgan.

21

They drove in tandem to the bed and breakfast. He was ahead of Eve, but Morgan no longer watched for her lights in his mirror. Buildings loomed around him like movie replicas, and the barn, pinpricked in light, reminded him of his sister's old doll house.

Their room took up the entire second floor of the barn and it was crammed with knick-knacks. Eve trailed her fingers along the spines of books and examined pots and jars. When she came to the king-size brass bed, she lifted a corner of the heavy quilt and admired the stitching.

"It's exquisite," she exclaimed. "This quilt has probably been handed down for generations."

Morgan stared at the quilt and wished he was back in his own apartment or even back at the farm. Eve begged him to come out onto the balcony and watch the stars.

"I don't understand what we're doing," he said.

"I don't either," Eve replied.

On the balcony, she leaned her head on his shoulder and stared into the sky. They didn't talk much, but when they got into bed, they held each other.

In the morning, they were tender. Eve planted kisses

on his chest and didn't resist when he raised her haunches and brought his mouth up between her legs. He caught sight of himself in the mirror, his red hair seemed violent against her pale white thighs.

Hours passed, and it seemed as if they would never leave the bed, but then a high-pitched voice called up the stairs. It was their host announcing the arrival of home-baked blueberry muffins. Eve dived off the bed and tangled in the quilt as she tried to flatpack between bed frame and floor. When she failed, she curled into a ball and rocked with suppressed laughter.

"Sorry, we slept late," Morgan called back. "Could you leave the muffins down there?"

"Eat them while they're still warm," the woman said. "I'll be back in a little while to freshen the room."

Her footsteps receded, and Eve clambered back onto the bed. She was holding her body as if her ribs hurt; she said she hadn't laughed like that in years.

"Reprobate," he said. "Do you think she heard us...you know, being vocal?"

"Do you mean having sex? I'm pretty sure that's legal. We did pay for the room."

I paid for the room, he thought, but didn't say.

"Muffins are here," Eve imitated, still on the verge of laughter. "She's probably dying to get in and clean. I can sympathize with that."

Wrapped in the quilt, Eve trailed downstairs and retrieved the muffins while Morgan made coffee. They ate on the bed, heedless of crumbs, and he told her about a silversmith on the island who made decorative bells, each with a signature sound.

"How lovely," she said. "This whole morning was lovely. But it doesn't change things."

"I've booked two nights. We still have time."

"I'm sorry. I thought you understood. I have to stay with Jess now. I need to be able to say, with a clear conscience, that I slept at her house. I'm sorry."

"That's why you wanted to come in two cars?"

Eve began to gather her things. He heard her in the bathroom brushing her teeth and then the thump of her suitcase being dragged down the stairs. She was halfway to her car when he caught up with her.

"Don't do this," he begged.

"I have to do this," she replied. "Will you stay on for the second night alone?"

"What do you care?" he asked, folding his arms and denying her a farewell hug.

He didn't wait to see her leave. Back in the room, everything reminded him of Eve: the quilt on the floor, the empty coffee mugs, her towel draped over a chair. There was no way he could stay here another night. He packed and went in search of their host who said she didn't give refunds and he'd be charged for the second night unless she got a late booking.

Traffic was slow as he joined the main road that ran past the ferry. He glimpsed Eve's car and accelerated past before he was spotted. He found the silversmith without much trouble. Signs on the main road pointed down a lane which dead-ended at a home-come-studio. The artist was an elfin man called James who wore several of his creations around his neck. He took Morgan through his creative process from start to finish, chiming whenever he moved.

The bells were surprising. A delicate one patterned with ferns rang deeply, while a dragon-shaped creation tinkled like a stream. James shrugged; apparently, the tone or character of each bell was beyond his artistic control. Morgan asked him to wrap the bell with the fern design which would be a perfect gift if he ever needed a final grand gesture.

Eve must have felt lonely waiting for the ferry, since she texted twice before she even left the island. One message admonished him for not saying goodbye properly and the other claimed it didn't have to be this way.

Morgan didn't respond to either message; she might be sorry now, but soon she'd be laughing with Jess over the muffin story. He would be a footnote, a crack in the union between husband and wife that could be plastered over and forgotten.

He wished now that he had never been inside her house. He should not have seen the photo of Luke, glimpsed the green love seat, or peered through the window of her private retreat. He should have kept himself separate and safe.

It took him hours to get home. While Eve's ferry sailed without incident, his was plagued by technical challenges and delays. He fell into bed past midnight and woke to find a rambling message from Eve. Her exit from the island had been hellish. The ferry ride had been choppy, and she got food poisoning from some chowder she'd eaten at the dock. She threw up all night and still felt tearful and weak. She hated how they left things; Jess was concerned about her state of mind.

Morgan went to work but didn't bother unpacking; the stolen bird feeder would lie on his floor for weeks. In the days that followed, he felt mostly numb. But on bad days, Eve seemed to live in his head. When he didn't respond to her texts, she began a campaign of veiled messages sent to the writing group but intended for him. She wrote about creative struggles, a lack of motivation, the melancholy that had her in its grip.

To give his own life purpose, Morgan took accrued sick leave and flew to Madison on the weekend of his parents' move. As he drove west from the airport, his thoughts drifted to Eve and the writing reunion planned for early next year. He wondered if he would go; he might have no choice if Zoe decided it would be good for the magazine.

Lost in thought, Morgan missed the turn-off to the farm. When he realized his error, he made no effort to correct course. It was only when he stopped for gas, that he admitted to himself where he was going.

It was almost dusk when he entered the quiet street where Eve's clapboard home nested between ranch-style brick houses. Even with a moody November sky, he could make out her ferns, resilient despite an early snow.

There were two vehicles parked in the drive. One was Eve's sedan and the other was a truck with Minnesota plates. With no clear plan on how he might lure Eve out, Morgan drove by at a crawl and then circled the block. On his second pass, he parked where he could see Eve's front door in his side view mirror.

The path appeared icy and the wind chime stirred restlessly on its hook. Morgan was hungry; gas station snacks were no substitute for real food. Next to him on the passenger seat was the box with the silver bell; he imagined giving it to Eve and saying he could outlast the winter if there was hope. He chewed his last donut hole and hunkered down to wait.

An hour passed and patience was rewarded when Eve surfaced in a long coat with wrap-around scarf. She got in her car and drove off in the opposite direction. Morgan waited thirty seconds then followed. She was an easy mark, driving well below the speed limit as if preoccupied; when she parked outside a grocery store, he parked ten bays over and watched her go inside.

He found her in the dried goods section, but hung back as she was talking with a stranger in slim-fit jeans. The woman twirled, while Eve ran a hand down her leg in the manner of a seamstress checking for a good fit. They walked together down one aisle and into the next. Morgan shadowed them but stayed out of sight.

At the check-out, a female cashier stepped out from behind her register and all three women embraced. Eve paid for her modest purchase of coffee beans and left the two women talking. Morgan waited and then went to a different register and paid for his sandwich. Impossible to reveal himself now; he would seem like a stalker.

This time when he drove past Eve's house, the curtains were shut and a soft light emanated from within. The truck was still there, so he had to assume Luke was staying the night. All he could do was find a motel and get the hell out of there the following day.

Later, when he lay fully clothed on a sagging mattress in a barely adequate motel, he thought of the farm with longing. Tom would be acting the part of responsible son; Faith would be tending her kids; his parents would be saying goodbye to the only place they had ever lived as a couple. He should be there with them.

In the morning, he left early and took a last swing past Eve's home. He expected it to be quiet, the occupants locked in slumber, but the side gate was open and Luke was loading a cooler and chairs into his truck. Eve was there in sunglasses she didn't need, and she had a bag slung over one shoulder. When their truck roared into life, Morgan swore and followed them out of the city.

They drove in a south-easterly direction. From a few cars back, he could see the outline of their heads. Eve faced the side window. Once, she disappeared altogether, and Morgan pictured an intimate sexual act, but she bobbed back up almost immediately as if she'd retrieved something from her bag.

When the truck turned off the highway and took minor roads, it was harder to stay hidden. Several times, he had to guess at turnings as they wove through a series of half-breath towns. They stopped, at last, on a lake front where Luke went into a cabin to get two coffees and what looked like cinnamon rolls. Eve took one of the cups but shook her head at the pastry. She had something in the crook of her arm, and she wandered away from Luke towards the dock that pointed into the lake like a stubby finger.

Morgan idled his car and wondered if they were going fishing. Luke had set up chairs on the dock and Eve was perched on the cooler.

They seemed to be engaged in a tense conversation, but it was like watching a play and being too far away to hear any dialogue.

Then the scene changed abruptly. Eve walked to the far end of the dock and Luke followed. She held out a container, fish bait Morgan presumed, and began to shake its contents out over the frigid water. When Luke put his hands over hers and joined in the ritual, Morgan put his foot on the gas.

He rammed the accelerator so hard his tires raked the gravel, and Eve looked over in his general direction. He raced back down the narrow lanes, cursing himself for being such an idiot. Not fish bait; that was obvious now. He'd intruded on a private ceremony, a memorial to someone or something that had nothing to do with him.

22

Morgan drove at a reckless speed as if to expunge his presence. But as he crossed the line that separated Minnesota from Wisconsin, a line that offered him immunity, he slowed down and gathered his thoughts.

His visit had been mistimed, but his intention had been noble. He had wanted to let Eve know that he would wait, that he would endure her silences, that he was stronger than he looked. If the circumstances had been different, he would have given her the bell as a symbol of his fidelity. Besides, no real harm had been done; Eve didn't even know about his mistimed visit.

With redemption in mind, Morgan took note of nature's beauty as he drove with purpose towards his parents' farm. When he arrived, everyone was outside. Tom had his sleeves rolled up and was carrying a large piece of furniture with Jerry; Faith was playing chase with the twins; his parents were examining items laid out on a long table.

They looked up as his car came down the drive, but no one moved to greet him. For a moment, he thought he wasn't welcome, but then Faith surged forward and gave him a hug.

"Better late than never," she said. "The moving truck's almost full."

"What's all this?" he asked, pointing at the table.

"Garage sale. We had a bunch of people yesterday. Tom advertised it all over town. He's been great. He's flying them to Florida first class; Mom's quite excited."

"Well, isn't he the hero," Morgan muttered, but then he remembered his crime and said he was glad things had gone so well.

"I wish you had been here," said Faith, "but I suppose we didn't need you after all."

He greeted his parents, and then he pushed Jerry aside so he could carry the dresser with Tom.

"Where are we going with this?" he asked.

"Are you sure you can manage?" drawled his brother. "We're taking it all the way down to the curb."

But halfway there, it was Tom who needed to rest.

"Why are we doing this anyway?" asked Morgan.

"Mom's idea, if you can believe that. It was the first piece of furniture they had as a married couple. Dad found it on a sidewalk and Mom wants it gone the same way."

"She's not usually that sentimental," Morgan said, opening a drawer and peering inside.

"It's empty, idiot. We checked. What are you looking for anyway?"

"There was a photo of Mom holding me as a baby outside a hospital. Do you know the one I mean?"

"I do, but that wasn't you in the photo," Tom said, not meeting his eye.

"What do you mean? It had to be."

"You're smart; figure it out. Not my story to tell."

Dinner was torture. Morgan looked at his mother so often she asked if she had food in her teeth. He apologized as Tom kicked him under the table. When their parents were safely upstairs, Morgan cornered Faith and told her about the photo and Tom's cryptic words.

"Do you know anything about it?" he asked.

"When I was pregnant with the twins, Mom hinted at a lost child. I assumed she meant a miscarriage."

"And you didn't ask questions?"

"Too awkward. But she got sad each February, remember? And there was the time she went away.

"What time?"

"You were young. She had some sort of collapse. I stayed with friends, but Tom had to look after you."

"What are you talking about?"

"She wasn't away long. We were supposed to act like nothing happened. I think Mom saw it as a weakness. Poor Dad; he never knew how to comfort her. Jerry may be bad at enforcing rules, but he's the first one to sit down and ask the twins how they feel. Hey, finish these dishes, will you? I need to check on my kids."

Morgan let the water drain from the sink and stared at the rust stain that had got the better of his mother over so many years. He wished he could ask her directly, and wondered what Eve would have said or done in his shoes. He didn't even know if the dead child was a girl or a boy.

Then he thought of his mother's response when he'd been bullied about his hair. She had been so angry, but had she also been terrified? And what about her horror at seeing Sideways' body in Morgan's bed? Should that be cast in a different light too? He felt his childhood shift by several seismic degrees.

It was a relief when he left the farm and returned to his single existence. Too much had happened in the course of a few days. It was easier to forget about it and focus on his New Mexico trip. He got his truck serviced, made a packing list, researched story ideas, paid attention to long-term weather reports and planned and re-planned his route. He would take several days to get there, do the interview with Savannah, shadow her, then take time for himself before returning to Savannah's for Christmas. He planned to be home again before the new year.

A few days before his departure, a postcard arrived from Eve showing a cityscape of bleeding colors. She was aware of his travel plans because Savannah had posted about his visit on the writing retreat thread. The message was brief: *Travel well. Miss me a little. I'm breaking apart. Don't let Savannah talk you out of…us.*

On the day of his departure, Zoe produced gummy bears and a stack of notebooks, while Rob handed him a well-thumbed copy of *New Mexico After Dark*. He threw the gifts into his truck and gave a thumbs up when Rob pretended to smash a bottle on his fender. The plastic bottle bounced off the truck's hood; as Morgan drove away, he saw his friend retrieve the gag for yet another day.

With a full tank of gas, clothes for all weathers, and enough snacks to last until the Oregon border, Morgan felt almost light-hearted. Behind him lay complication and heartache, ahead more than fifteen hundred miles of road. He would pay attention to the scenery, get a feel for each place, but mostly he would sink into the pleasure of being in motion and not yet arrived.

Five hours later, butt-sore and eager to get out of the truck, he had crossed the boredom threshold and run through his CDs. The radio had been disappointing. He had no idea so many religious stations in Idaho disguised their message in soft rock.

He was almost relieved when a posse of Harley Davidsons swarmed him at a gas station. He parked out of their way and approached the leader, curious about the purpose for their ride. He wished he had on something cooler than Tom's old windbreaker and the wool hat with the logo that Zoe had insisted he wear.

The lead rider was friendly - a mild-mannered engineer from the Midwest who explained that the trip was a memorial ride to honor their dead friend. The group agreed to photographs and gave their backstory along with several juicy quotes. Story number one was in the bag.

By the time Morgan crossed into New Mexico, he had enough copy to keep Zoe off his back for weeks. The last story, about a woman walking the length of the country relying on the kindness of strangers, was the perfect feel-good ending to a travel series. If the interview with Savannah went half as well, he'd be employee of the month when he got back.

He recognized Savannah's house from a distance. Who else would live in a spaceship in the middle of sage? As he got closer, the spaceship became a medium-sized adobe with rounded edges, orbital turrets, and brightly painted doors. Set against the bruise of red and purple mountains, it was the perfect place for a muse.

He was still taking shots of the exterior when Savannah emerged from the house along with a carnival dog. Part-Bichon and part-Chihuahua, the formerly white animal had been streaked pink and wore a gold collar.

"You're here," Savannah said, hugging him in a cloud of gardenia. "Welcome to my humble abode."

When Morgan came up for air, she held him at arm's length and studied him as if he was a painting. She no longer had blonde curls; instead, her hair was short, ragged and jet black.

"You look exhausted," she said. "Leave your bags. I want to show you around."

They walked through a blue wooden door into a courtyard where red roses idled in pots like nodding somnambulists. Savannah called them 'her babies' and said they needed constant feeding and must be brought inside on frosty nights. As he wove between the favored children and dodged the dog turds that dotted the gravel, Morgan wondered what that had to do with him.

"Ready?" she asked. "Welcome to Savannah-land!"

She flung open the back door, and the first thing Morgan noticed was a bench draped in orange velvet holding a row of witch-like dolls.

Most of the dolls wore capes and pointed hats, but a few had tangled, knotted hair as if they had blown backwards through a hedge. At their feet lay an artful arrangement of skulls, bones and brooms.

"My Halloween tableaux," she explained. "I liked it so much I kept it going."

Morgan spun slowly. There was a striped sofa in one corner, a pink dog bed that resembled a throne, and a series of animal figures set in alcoves around the room. Of these, the most startling was a vixen carrying a harp.

"It's quite something," he said.

They passed through a relatively normal kitchen and entered a dusky bedroom where a ceiling mural showed naked cherubs wearing stilettos. An electric guitar, strung on a heavy chain, hung from a cherub's leg over a massive canopy bed. Tiny stairs led up to this creation.

"The steps are for Pinky," Savannah explained, as the little dog climbed up on cue and glared at Morgan. "He's possessive," she laughed, obviously delighted.

She flung open a closet, as if Morgan had asked to see her clothes, and inside were suits and dresses more suitable for cabaret than daily wear. On the top shelf, a series of wigs were draped over placid head dummies.

"Damian's workspace is through there," she waved a vague hand. "I'll let him show you that; he's fussy about his gear. Let's go see my office."

Office was not the right word. The desk was barely visible under stacks of magazines and every inch of wall was covered in images.

"It's one giant collage," Morgan observed.

"Exactly. Stay here long enough, and you become part of the design."

"I feel disoriented," he admitted, picturing his photo spread with the caption: Blinded by Color.

"Want to see where you'll sleep? It's our favorite room in the house."

The room was actually a loft with a simple mattress on the floor and a side table piled high with fairy tale books. The bed was unmade, and there were signs of recent activity; a large red dildo, anatomical, sat to attention on the floor. Savannah swooped down and grabbed the cock and balls.

"Whoops. I meant to put that away earlier," she giggled. "We come up here because it has the best views. When it rains; the whole place smells of sage. We have clean sheets somewhere. Get your bags; I'll open beers.

23

Outside, the sky was subdued and the mountains had become dark shadows. Morgan swept crumbs off the seat of his truck and shook out the cooler. He was in no hurry. A coyote called across the valley, and Morgan felt an urge to call right back. When he joined Savannah, she was sitting out on the porch with Pinky on her lap. She had lit a brazier and was rolling a joint.

"Want one?" she asked. "Or we can share."

"I haven't smoked in forever; it will probably go straight to my head."

It was pleasant to sit there with a view of the distant mountains; gradually, he let go of the miles and even his purpose in being there. All that mattered was the glowing tip passed back and forth between them in a gentle wave.

"Damian will cook once he gets home," Savannah said, after a long silence. "This is a good time to ask me your questions. Once he's home, I'll be distracted."

"Can't we do it in the morning?"

"Honey, you haven't seen me in the morning. I sleep late, and then it's straight out for coffee. Besides, I don't think we'll have time. We hit the road early afternoon, and I haven't even started packing."

"Hit the road? I thought I was going to shadow you for a week?"

"Damian picked up new clients in Texas; it was all last-minute. We need to wine and dine them. Get your notebook, or whatever you use, and I'll go ahead and roll us a fresh one."

Morgan chose to record the interview on his phone. It would mean hours of transcription, but there was no way he could take coherent notes in his current state. He would probably create an unofficial version for Rob: *Reader I Did Inhale.*

As the interview rolled forward and stars slipped out of the darkening sky, a picture of the Muse began to form. She helped artists of all stripes. If a painter was blocked, she would pry him or her loose; if a writer fixated on a blank page, she was the one who stirred up creative juices. She had anecdotes in spades, along with visuals since the artists often paid in kind. Zoe would eat this up.

"That's all I've got," Savannah said, at last.

"Not your first rodeo," Morgan acknowledged.

"Interviewers tend to ask similar questions," she said, patting his leg. "By the way, Damian has shot me from every conceivable angle and in every imaginable pose; as long as you credit him, you can take your pick."

"How long will you be gone?"

"A week tops, but I'll make it worth your while with weed and cash. You'll love it here. You can write up the interview and detox from Eve. I was going to ask, but it's written all over your face."

He would have protested, but Damian arrived and Pinky leaped off Savannah's lap to greet his master. The man was smaller even than his photo implied and his dark features gave him the look of a satyr.

"Sorry I'm late," he said. "The Cantina was busy, and then I ran into Salvador and we had beers. I got take-out in the end; it was simpler."

Damian handed a brown paper bag to Savannah and they disappeared into the house. Abandoned, Pinky cocked his head and then his leg. As Morgan looked down at his damp shoe, he wondered how he would ever survive the week.

He would learn soon enough that Pinky ruled the household and only Savannah knew his needs. He would also discover it was impossible to drink enough beer to forget Eve and that tacos made his hosts horny. Before the night took this uncomfortable turn, Damian revealed he was a former rock star who met Savannah when she pushed her way into his dressing room at a gig.

"She was a force," Damian admitted. "Still is. She joined the tour and acted like she belonged. I wrote some damn good songs that week."

He showed off his collection of guitars and offered to play some riffs, but Savannah called time on the party. She said she needed beauty sleep, but it was clearly the furthest thing from her mind. Morgan heard every grunt and scream associated with her four orgasms. Even Pinky took refuge upstairs.

Morgan slept late. When he made it downstairs, Savannah had just returned from her favorite coffee haunt and Damian had done all the packing. There were enough bags for a two-week vacation.

"It's important that you bring Pinky up to your bed in the morning," Savannah said. "He's used to mummy and daddy kisses."

By the time he waved them off, Morgan was exhausted. He slumped in a chair while his charge hopped onto the pink dog bed and dangled his head over the side.

"Don't think you can charm me," Morgan warned. "You have serious problems. That bed for starters."

But by day's end, Morgan warmed to his charge and figured out a rough schedule that would help manage the week. He would transcribe interviews in the morning and write in the afternoons. Evenings would be given over to whatever stimulants he desired. That left lunchtime for walks with the dog.

Over the next few days, he more or less followed this schedule. He finished three travel pieces, transcribed the interview with Savannah and neutered his desire for Eve by smoking a lot of pot. Then he fired off an email to Savannah and asked what time they would be back.

Her reply came a day later. There had been an issue in the warehouse where Damian stored his guitars and they'd been forced to fly to Georgia. It made no sense to come home and leave again for Christmas; they would not be coming back until the new year.

It was the tone that annoyed Morgan the most; not even a suggestion of an apology, just an assumption that his time meant nothing and their needs came first.

"It would serve her right if you upped and left," Faith said, when he complained to her over the phone.

"I would if it wasn't for Pinky."

"You could do a story about that: journalist held hostage by an eight-pound dog."

He felt better when he hung up the phone. Faith was a good listener, but she was also stressed by the prospect of her in-laws for Christmas and a mountain of tasks. At least in New Mexico, he could do his own thing.

"We need to mix it up," he told Pinky. "No more sequestering at the house. Let's do a real hike."

They drove out through town, past the dog park and into more rugged terrain where Pinky stuck his head out of the window and sniffed the air.

"I can see through your ears you know," Morgan told him. "You look like a bat."

They parked at a trailhead and walked up a path among pinyon pine. Morgan kept up a brisk pace, but Pinky matched him step-for-step so that by the time they reached the overlook the dog had earned Morgan's respect.

They sat down on a rock and gazed out over the city that spread before them in a neat geometry of lives. It was peaceful, until a pair of crows flew too close and Pinky lunged at them, barking hysterically; Morgan only just saved him from going over the edge.

"My life would have been over too," he said. "Your mother would have killed me."

The hike back down took half the time. At the bottom, Pinky quenched his thirst in a stream, but Morgan fought dry mouth as they drove a new route back to town. Minor roads took them through villages, and Morgan spied a café with blue shutters that served home-made burritos.

Inside, the place had a cheerful vibe with bright plastic tablecloths and Native crafts arranged on a table along one wall. The woman who served him had dark hair in two long plaits. While he waited for his order, he looked at the leather pouches, flutes, dream catchers and paintings laid out for sale. Each price tag was written in pencil as if nothing was fixed. He made a plan to return without Pinky and see if he could haggle some bargains.

He took the food to go, along with several bottles of water, and ate as he drove. Bits of food fell in his lap, and by the time they reached the mailbox at the end of Savannah's drive, Morgan's entire pant leg was damp with Pinky's spittle. He collected a pile of letters and two packages and drove the last few hundred yards with Pinky on his lap.

"What do you suppose she wants?" he asked his companion, when he found a letter addressed to himself from Eve. "She's not doing a very good job of leaving me alone, is she? Do you find that ominous or a good sign?"

Morgan read the letter twice then took it outside to lay on the brazier. He watched it writhe and curl like a fortune-telling fish in the still-warm ashes.

Apparently, it was hard to mend a marriage. There were steps forward and steps back, reflexes of shame as well as regret. Eve's therapist said she needed more sleep and better nutrition. She was eating kale and popping vitamins and had invested in a green powder that was supposed to save her life. How did one know if a marriage was over?

Later that night, with his feet tangled in not-so-clean sheets, Morgan listened to the brewing storm and thought about Savannah's version of Eve. She'd called her a narcissist, which made him think of the expression about the pot calling the kettle black. Then she'd gone further and said that Eve was toying with him; Morgan was like a puppy with a rock tied around his neck.

"That wasn't a nice thing to say, was it Pinky?" he asked, but the dog only grunted. "I don't think your mother is capable of appreciating Eve."

A rumble of thunder set Pinky barking, and he trotted downstairs. Morgan found him with his nose jammed under the sofa. But he wasn't trying to hide; Pinky was hunting a mouse. Morgan could see that one of the creature's legs was broken, but he was still alive. He got an egg box from the kitchen and moved the sofa out a quarter-inch. He held Pinky away and scooped up the injured mouse.

The moon was almost full; he carried the creature out through the courtyard and into the sage where he tipped him into a sandy hollow. He could see the animal's heart ricochet under the matted fur. Something would hasten his end - a bird or a coyote more skilled at killing – and surely, that would be a blessing.

Blessing - a word from Eve's letter. She was actively dreading Christmas. Her sister had been vile and her mother had invited Luke in hope of a reconciliation. Her family was a dysfunctional mess. Morgan didn't know how lucky he was to be alone; he should count it as a blessing.

24

When Morgan returned to bed, he found Pinky snoring under the covers. He moved him to the edge of the mattress, but pulled him close again to feel the rise and fall of his chest. His heart ached with pressures old and new, and it took a long time to fall asleep.

When morning leaned in through the un-curtained window, his senses exploded with sage. Savannah was right, this was the best spot in the house; it was a new day, and anything was possible.

He made coffee - always coffee, as if life could be measured by the number of cups he consumed - while Pinky curled up on his dog bed, resentful about the theft of his mouse. Morgan ruffled the dog's head as he passed and took his coffee out to the courtyard where the morning light glanced off the snow-dusted mountains and turned them a soft pink.

There had been snow in Minnesota too, according to Eve, adding to her sense of entrapment. She felt as if there was no escape; she wondered if all relationships fractured in ways that were indeterminate and messy.

There was nothing in the house for breakfast, so he

put on layers and drove solo to the café with the blue shutters. The woman with the braids was deep in conversation with a supplier behind a bead curtain, so he idled by the craft table and picked up one of the flutes he could not afford.

The wood was smooth, fine-grained, and the artist had carved an eagle near the top of the chamber; the bird would take metaphorical flight whenever the flute was played. He blew a tentative note just as the bead curtain made a percussive sound.

"It takes practice," the woman said.

He tried again and produced a rushing sound. She laughed and took the flute from him, blowing a clear low note followed by a series of trills.

"Are you looking for anything special?" she asked, laying the flute back on the shelf.

"Coffee," he said. "I need coffee and a burrito."

"If it's straight up coffee you want, help yourself from the carafe while I work on the burrito."

He ate at a table near the register and chatted with the woman while she arranged pastries on the counter. He told her he was a journalist and that this was his first time in New Mexico. He needed input on places he should visit.

"My dark face means I'm a native?" she asked.

"I'm sorry, I shouldn't have assumed…"

"I'm teasing you. There's a church nearby that's famous from a Georgia O'Keefe painting. Other than that, you should visit the Pueblo and maybe the Hanuman Temple. If it's local knowledge you want, there are guide books under the counter."

He studied the titles then pulled two paperbacks from the shelves. One looked dry, a potted history of the region, but the other was full of photos. The Pueblo, built in the thirteenth century, had been continuously inhabited up to the present day.

"You can borrow that," she told him. "Bring it back when you visit the church or drop it off at my home."

She handed him a business card with her name and address: Isabella Martin, Artist and Café Owner. He asked if she would use her creative eye to help him choose one of the pouches for a friend.

"What is this friend like?" she asked.

"Creative; mysterious; infuriating," he said.

She laughed and came around from behind the counter. After some consideration, she chose a tan-colored pouch with a hummingbird design picked out in beads. The drawstring was adorned with tiny green feathers.

"Twice a year, hummingbird visits," she told him. "We're a stop along the way, not a final destination. We honor their presence and their necessary departure."

He bought the pouch then asked directions to the post office where he chose a postcard of Taos in the snow. Then he wrote, word for word, what Isabella had said about the hummingbird's visit. The bell fit perfectly inside the pouch, and he wrapped it all with protective padding and addressed the package to Eve. The gift, along with the words, would be open to interpretation.

That Sunday, Morgan went to the church that Isabella had mentioned. He recognized the building from college posters as well as a commemorative stamp produced to honor the artist's origins in Sun Prairie, Wisconsin. Faith had bought a whole sheet back then in case they became valuable one day.

The church was full, mostly with Hispanic congregants, but the priest was white and Scottish and difficult to understand. Afterwards, when Morgan asked where he came from in Scotland, the man beamed his pleasure.

"Glasgow," he said. "But here they think I'm Irish."

There was no time to get his story; a toothless man with leathery skin prodded Morgan from behind, and he was forced to move away. He walked to the café where he found Isabella smoking outside; he asked if she knew anything about the priest.

"Nothing," she replied, offering him an unfiltered cigarette which he declined. "Did you see the painting?"

"No. I assumed her paintings would all be in museums or galleries."

"Not a painting by O'Keeffe. I mean the one in the back room that's supposed to have miraculous properties."

"No one mentioned a painting. Do you believe in that kind of thing?"

"This town is full of superstitions," she said. "The longer I'm here, the more I appreciate the old ways."

"How did you end up here?"

"There was a man," she said. "And step-kids."

"But no longer?"

"No longer," she agreed, stubbing out her cigarette on the café wall. "I've found another book on the Pueblo. Come on inside."

The new book focused on Pueblo ceremonies and would be a perfect resource for his Christmas story. He thanked her and was about to ask what she thought of ceremonies when a wave of customers came in from the church. Before she was swallowed up, he got directions for the Hanuman temple.

But temple was too grand a name for a long wooden building full of hippies on the outskirts of town. He found his presence was accepted without question, and he was welcomed with a cup of chai. Someone directed him downstairs where he confronted a life-sized Hanuman. The monkey god was draped in silk and reclined on one elbow. In front of him sat a ceremonial bowl of fruit.

A skinny man in white began to pump a music box, while another man waved a candelabra of lights. The room filled up with worshippers who chanted in a foreign tongue. In the midst of this ceremony, a small boy wandered up to the statue and filched a banana. No one, least of all Hanuman, seemed to mind. Morgan scribbled notes, took a few sly photos and left before the incense choked him.

Back at Savannah's, Pinky appeared to be in a sulk and had left a puddle by the back door. Mindful of his promise, Morgan clipped on the dog's lead and took him for a walk through the neighborhood. Here and there, land had been cleared for development and there were houses scattered along some of the finished roads. Outside the nearest house, a diminutive woman thumped a door mat with the end of a broom. She waved when she saw Morgan.

"I like your spaceship house," he called out.

"You want to see inside?" she asked. "My son is the architect. Everything is recycled, even the rain."

Her accent was Austrian, he thought, and her olive skin and white hair reminded him of his mother. She introduced herself as Zeena and ordered him to leave Pinky on the porch.

"Rudolph does not like dogs," she explained.

He wondered if Rudolph was her husband, but he turned out to be a fat cat who slumbered on a chair in the living room and hissed when Morgan approached.

"Tea or coffee?" Zeena asked. "I'm a tea drinker, but Americans often prefer coffee."

As the tea brewed, she took him on a tour of the house and pointed out the re-used products. There were tires in the walls, mud in the plaster, bottle ends transformed into windows. She even grew vegetables inside. Morgan thought of his own messy apartment and his failure to recycle even on a minor scale.

They drank their tea from delicate china cups, and Zeena explained she was half-English but linked to other places as well. She had just returned from Israel, having gone there to witness the suffering on both sides.

"I'm not Jewish," she said, "but I love their traditions. I was born in Germany. I heard the voice of Hitler when I was a child."

"What was that like?" he asked.

"At the time, not memorable. Afterwards, terrifying."

He told her about his visit to the Hanuman Temple and the church. She said she thought most traditions had something to offer. She herself held gatherings to mark the Sabbath and the people who came practiced different religions. She pressed him to stay for a second cup of tea, but Pinky was shivering out on the porch. When he shook her hand, she held on to it and looked deep into his eyes. She told him life was a gift and he should use it well.

He thought about her words as he walked back along the road. What did it mean to use a life well? How did one measure such a thing? He asked Faith what she thought when he called her that evening.

"I think you must be lonely to call me this much. What are you going to do on Christmas Day?"

"I'll work late on Christmas Eve, so I'll probably sleep late. I'm not that bothered, to be honest."

"I'm envious. Jerry's colleagues are coming tonight and then his family tomorrow. I'm going to start drinking now and not stop. Call me if you find yourself at a loose end."

25

The next morning, snow fell thick and fast which meant the Pueblo's ochre buildings would contrast well in any of Morgan's photographs. He shoveled a path for Pinky and then got to work on a rough outline for his story using the facts he had gleaned from the books. After that, he checked his camera and recorder, chose a fresh notebook and located several working pens. Finally, he made a pot of soup that would last several days and removed the excess snow from his truck.

It was only then that he thought about the roses. Too late; if he brought them in now, the mess would outweigh any benefit. He banked the fire, filled Pinky's bowl with kibble, and set off for the Pueblo in the late afternoon.

The roads were packed with snow, and he felt the constant threat of slide under his wheels. When he turned onto Pueblo land there was already a long line of cars. He would be one of the last to make it into the parking lot, but at least it would assure his easy exit.

He walked in under an archway and followed a group of locals along the line of the adobe wall. It was cold enough to see his breath; he was glad he had dressed warmly.

They turned a corner and he let the others move ahead so he could get a shot of the church. The walkway was lined with candles in brown paper bags, and two giant Christmas trees stood to attention on either side of massive wooden doors. He took several shots that were a blur of sunset and candle, and then he entered the church.

Inside, the mood was carnival; people chatted and laughed as if waiting for their favorite band. Mary, mother of Jesus, held center-stage in three-dimensional form. On the wall behind her, Jesus wandered a landscape of native people amidst a harvest of squash and corn.

Morgan chose a seat near the back and soaked in the atmosphere. After a while, the crowd became restive and voices pitched louder as the starting time came and went. Late arrivals squeezed into already heaving pews. A white couple with a baby moved closer to a heater, and their seats were taken by four Pueblo women.

At last, a Spanish-looking priest appeared at the lectern and the crowd grew quiet; he apologized for the delay and told them they were waiting for the bishop. Two Indian men in jeans approached the statue of Mary and conferred in loud whispers with the priest.

Bishop-be-damned, the men began to manhandle Mary. Large brown hands enveloped her waist and hoisted her into a processional chair. They fussed, like bridal attendants, while several women kissed the hem of her dress. Morgan made detailed notes for his Seattle readers.

The bishop arrived at last, old and white, and spoke of the time-honored ways of the Pueblo. But Mary's attendants grew restless. They seemed unable to leave her alone, as if the bishop was a distraction and Mary the main act. A hymn followed, but the choir that perched in an upper gallery sang out-of-sync with the organ.

At long last, the procession began. Down the aisle swung Mary, held aloft by four men who bumped into pews and stopped to chat with their friends.

When Mary reached the wooden doors, the congregation rose and followed her out to the courtyard where bonfires burned bright against the snow. The frigid air clamped throats and steamed jackets but Mary processed forward oblivious to the cold. Then cheers rang out and young men fired antique weapons into the air.

Morgan took photos and kept his voice recorder running to catch the ambient sounds. Part of him wanted to make fun of the entire event, but another part yearned to belong with this rag-tag group of people. A story formed that he wanted to call 'Madonna Rules' only he knew Zoe would find that too cute.

He drove back to Savannah's in a trance, images crowding his brain. When he began to write, he found it easy to weave those intimate scenes from the church with his prepared story. He filed the piece twenty minutes before deadline, and Zoe's response came within the hour: *You're not fired. This is good work. You may even get a bonus. I want you back at the Pueblo for New Year's Day.*

He celebrated with four shots of tequila on an almost-empty stomach. When he woke late on Christmas day, he was still on the sofa and the world was buried under a thick new layer of snow. He wondered if Eve would call and what she had thought of his present. He would keep his expectations low.

When his phone rang early that evening, he answered with hope, but it was only Savannah who was calling to speak to her dog. She warned of further delays. They'd be back January 2nd at the latest. Did he hate her? She promised to add zeros to his final dollar amount, and she told him the location of another stash of weed.

Morgan made no mention of his New Year's Day assignment, but implied he was tested by the delays and doing her a massive favor. When he hung up, he unearthed the new stash of weed and had just chosen a movie to watch, when his phone rang again.

"I have one minute," Eve said. "Thank you for the pouch and the bell. I didn't expect such precious gifts."

"Everyone likes to be remembered."

"I wanted to send you something too, but I ran out of time and didn't get to a post office. In the end, I put a package in a mail box and guessed at the postage."

"I don't think that works."

"I did my best. You have no idea what it's like here. My mother oozes disapproval and Luke is filled with self-righteous rage. My sister had the nerve to say I'd torn the family apart, but then she flirted with Luke all through dinner. It was my definition of hell."

"You chose it," Morgan said.

It took him a minute to realize Eve had hung up the phone. He turned the Tequila bottle upside down and licked the rim. Damn Savannah and her last-minute needs; damn Eve and her carelessness. All he wanted was a sign that he mattered. Was that too much to ask?

With Christmas over, the days passed with little shape or direction. It rained and the snow turned to slush. The roses released the last of their petals, and the tips of the mountains played hide and seek in the mist. Morgan slept late most mornings and stayed in sweats all day. He grew an embryonic beard and his hair became feral. He lived off whatever he could find in the freezer and finished the new batch of weed. Even Pinky began to ignore him.

It took a call from Zoe to turn things around. She needed him back in the office soon and now regretted giving him such a long leash. Even with the stories he had filed, there was a backlog of other work. If he didn't return soon, she'd have to hire someone else. He promised to write the new story within a day of the event and then return as soon as he could.

For the first time in several days, Morgan took Pinky for a walk and the cold air sobered him. When he got back, he took a long shower and shaved off his ridiculous beard. Then he went into town and bought fresh bread and enough vegetables to make another large batch of soup. He ate early and watched televised fireworks from a few remote time zones before he went to bed.

On New Year's Day, Morgan entered the Pueblo in lockstep with a burly cop whose buzz cut defied the season. He heard chanting and the low growl of drums. In the courtyard, bare-chested men in loin cloths stamped their feet and shook rattles. Some had animal pelts or dead birds at their waist, several wore their hair in traditional plaits, a few were close-shaven. Every one of them carried evergreen sprigs.

"What are they doing?" Morgan asked.

"Dance of the Turtle," replied the cop. "It marks the beginning of the year."

The dancers moved steadily from one side of the Pueblo to the other. The younger men, bent over from cold, had ribs that jutted out through pimpled skin, but the men in their thirties and forties stood upright. Strongest of all were the grandfathers whose chests and heads were held high. They faced each of the four directions and danced while their breath froze and their skin shone. When they were finished, they vanished into the Pueblo.

Morgan walked past the piles of ash and charcoal left over from the Christmas fires and tried to see where the dancers had gone. He was blocked by women wielding wooden paddles which they plunged into clay ovens to remove steaming loaves of bread. He glimpsed laden tables and understood there would be a feast to call in the year's good blessings. His story would practically write itself.

He drove back to Savannah's and began heating up a bowl of the previous night's soup. Unlike the people of the Pueblo, he had no rituals to call in the new year, but he too wanted a fresh start. He would begin by calling Eve and telling her he was sorry.

As soon as she answered the phone, Morgan launched into his apology. He had been insensitive and cold; of course, she hadn't had time to get him a proper gift. Could she please forgive him?

"I can't talk now," Eve said, when Morgan drew breath. "I'm not alone. I have a friend staying and we are enjoying a medicinal glass of wine."

"What friend?" he asked.

"Just a friend who's visiting family in Minneapolis. I can't tell you how good it feels to talk with someone who knows my story and doesn't judge."

Morgan jabbed the spoon against the base of the pan to stop the soup catching and splashed himself.

"Did you call for anything else?" Eve asked.

"Are you definitely going to the reunion?"

"Jess and I cooked it up together, so I'm duty bound."

"Were you ever going to ask me to come?"

"I didn't think I needed to ask."

He jabbed the spoon again and said she must be tired from all the Christmas drama.

"I'm not tired, are you?"

He heard the friend laugh and then Eve's request to fill their glasses and stoke the fire.

"I'll let you go," he said. "I have a story to file."

26

It wasn't his best work, but Zoe accepted the story and Morgan went to bed early and then spent several hours whispering into Pinky's long-suffering ear.

When Savannah returned the next day, she made good on her promise and gave him a fistful of dollars. She also demanded entertaining anecdotes about her dog, so Morgan spun a few yarns while Savannah rained kisses on Pinky's head. Then he confessed about the roses.

"Already saw them," she said. "Don't sweat it; they were a lot of work."

So much for her babies, he thought, as Savannah plonked Pinky back in his bed and strode off in the direction of her office. But at the doorway, she turned and asked a challenging question.

"Did you use your time wisely? Are you done with that ridiculous infatuation of yours?"

When he didn't reply, she rolled her eyes and disappeared into her office. He could hear her on the phone telling Damian to get sourdough bread and a fresh bottle of Tequila. No, she wasn't sure when Morgan was leaving. Yes, she thought he would be with them at least one more night. He trod away softly and packed his bags.

"There's no rush," Savannah said, half-heartedly, when he told her he was leaving. "Wait for Damian, at least. He should be back soon, although I did give him a long list of things to get at the store."

But Morgan didn't wait. He said goodbye to Pinky, hopped into his truck and sped off before Savannah could cause any delay. He took a small detour and arrived at the café to return Isabella's books. But the boy behind the counter said it was her day off, and she was most likely at home. He hesitated, but he chose to leave the books with a note of apology. The last thing he needed was another complication of the female kind.

The drive home was surgical, until snow turned to ice in northern Utah, and he was forced to stop for a second night. While the snow ploughs did their work, he lay awake on a mattress that felt as if it was made of straw. When he finally reached home, he slept for thirteen hours straight and woke in the middle of a day.

The apartment felt alien and everything in it was coated in a fine layer of dust. He shopped for food, started a load of laundry, spread dirt around with a damp cloth, and, at long last, hung the bird feeder. When he sorted his mail, he found a postcard from his mother that said simply: *Wish you were here.*

The picture was a typical beach scene. He called Faith to find out if the message was sincere. She laughed and said Margaret had always wanted to use that line. They loved Florida. John had taken to the place like a fish to water; he had joined a club of retired engineers and was hardly ever home. Margaret was busy as well with a church group and meals on wheels."

"Sounds horrendous," he said, "but I'm glad they are happy."

"How about you? Is it good to be home?"

"Jury's out," he said. "Nothing but chores in my immediate future.

His return to work was briefly triumphant. For two days, he basked in Zoe's approval over the Pueblo pieces and the three-page spread on Savannah. After that, she gave him a pile of overdue work and Rob went back to teasing him about his secret or imaginary love life.

Rob wasn't wrong. He had not been able to forget Eve, despite Savannah's scathing assessment and the piles of evidence that Eve's needs and emotions seesawed at his expense. He wondered what it was he hoped to gain in the relationship. Was he locked in some imaginary battle with Luke over possession of Eve?

As January lurched to a close and the writers' reunion drew near, Morgan was still not sure if he was going. Zoe had been lukewarm; she thought they had milked the story, and there were others issues for his journalistic attention. Despite this, Morgan told the group he would be there.

A typed letter had arrived from Eve. Her tone was impersonal; she was focused on home improvements and had hired a 'handyman' who was actually a woman. She was doing a modest bathroom re-model and transforming the basement. Anna was calm, efficient, and a good listener with ideas of her own. Her best feature, Eve wrote, was definitely her toolbelt.

Morgan had been on the point of contacting Jess for back-channel news when Eve called him. She wanted to meet at the Ukulele Café. He told her that it made no sense geographically, but Eve insisted. They needed to be *on the same page* before the reunion began.

"Can't you just say what you need to say over the phone?"

"I can tell you that it has been hellish. I can tell you Luke has been angry. I can tell you that I've hurt him badly, and I haven't known how to make it better."

"And where does that leave us?"

"I haven't been fair to you," Eve said, sounding desperate. "Can we just meet?"

In light of this conversation, Morgan made a strong case to Zoe. He implied that Savannah would be there at the reunion and that Gill was willing to go on record. Neither of these things were true, but he would cross that bridge when he got there.

When the day came, he dressed with deliberate lack of care. He chose tired jeans, boots with a split at the seam and a shirt that Eve had said made him look sallow. At the last minute, he added the hat he had worn in Taos.

He arrived at the café on time but remained in his truck. Eve was sitting on a stool by the window. She had straightened her hair; a blank sheet of sophistication had replaced unruly curls. She looked stiff, like a mannequin, and her face was too angular. When she noticed him, she gave a sad smile, the echo of an echo of joy; then, she unfurled and moved closer to the window.

When Eve splayed her fingers against the café window, Morgan got out of the truck and mirrored the gesture form his side. He could see faint circles under her eyes. As they moved sideways to the door, her silver pendant of intertwined roses swung like a pendulum pronouncing their fate.

She drew him inside and said it had been raining when she landed in Seattle, but as soon as she reached Tacoma it cleared. Over coffee, her story came out in fits and starts: Luke's rage; his slow corroding jealousy; the failure of their therapy sessions. He had moved out of the house and stopped paying bills, so she was fixing up the basement for a tenant. As Morgan listened, he understood that Luke had won nothing at all.

"Shall we go somewhere else to eat?" he asked, stilling her hands. "I feel as if the walls of this place are saturated with our sad story. How does Indian sound?"

They ate the buffet, and standing before mountains of rice and seas of dhal, Eve revealed she was the kind of person who wanted it all; he should know that about her. She ordered beer to *blur her edges*; Morgan had water.

"I'm living a soap opera," Eve complained. "My mother thinks divorce is a sin."

"Divorce?" he echoed.

"Something Luke mentioned at Christmas."

"I see."

"Do you? Then perhaps you can explain it to me. It's far too soon to talk of anything so final. No one in either of our families has ever gotten divorced."

"You'd be a trailblazer."

"Not funny."

"Do you want to stay married?" he asked.

"I want everyone to be happy. I want grief to end. I want flesh back on bones. I want the hurt I've inflicted to be undone. If you had seen Luke's face when he said he was moving out...he was a lost little boy."

"Nothing happens in a vacuum."

"My therapist says it has been a long time coming," Eve agreed. "Luke stopped going after three sessions. He said the therapist was on my side - as if there are sides in therapy. Despite that, he comes on weekends to finish the sanctuary."

They lapsed into silence after that, contemplating Luke's sacrifice, and Eve ordered another beer. Morgan longed to mention the scene at the lake and the ceremony he'd almost ruined. Instead, he asked how it felt to have Luke at their home.

"It's hard. There are so many memories. We've talked about selling, but I'm not ready to leave. If it wasn't for Anna, I'd be a total wreck."

Towards the end of the meal, she mentioned the other reason she had wanted to meet ahead of the retreat. Ruby, the massage therapist, was coming to Washington State with her friend. She'd invited them both to visit her cabin after the retreat.

"I thought you'd like to meet my friends," Eve said. "But you don't look happy."

"You didn't ask; you just assumed I'd be free."

"Well, aren't you?"

"That's not the point."

The ferry was half-empty, yet they remained in Morgan's truck for the duration of the ride. Eve prattled on about Ruby, but asked nothing about his time in New Mexico. She told him the cabin weekend would help her feel she existed outside all of the chaos. She was curious, too, about Ruby's extra-marital affair or relationship.

"How did they even meet?" Morgan asked.

"At a grocery store of all places. Apparently, Micheline complemented Ruby on her skin and asked if she would pose as a life model. Painting is her passion."

"And one thing led to another," he guessed.

"It's intriguing; we may have something to learn."

27

It was quiet when they arrived at the retreat site. There was no welcome party since it was off-season and they had hired the venue at a cheaper rate. Someone would cook meals and Gill would join them on the final day for the readings. Other than that, they were on their own.

Eve chose the same room as before, but this time Morgan was allowed into the loft and Jess would stay downstairs. He dumped his bags and watched through the bannisters as Eve folded her clothes into the drawers.

"I'm going to pick flowers for Jess," she said, when she was finished. "She'll be disappointed we aren't in the same room."

He asked if she wanted company, but Eve shook her head. He waited, but she never returned. Since the days were unscheduled, there was nothing to tie them together. When the others began to arrive, Morgan left the room and escaped down the wood-chip path to his old cabin.

The door was locked and the porthole window was obscured by lichen. He could just make out the picture, crooked again, and the edge of his desk. He had found something here – a younger, better version of himself.

Why had he let himself be distracted by a Buddha emblem and a spinning top?

He sat on the porch, ignoring the damp, and opened his laptop. As he read through the story he'd written at the first retreat, he felt almost tender towards his mother and more sympathetic to Tom. He looked for places he could soften the text and added details about the photograph. He wasn't sure what to do about the ending.

That evening, their first formal gathering went on too long; there was no one to stem lengthy check-ins. Eve had scraps of paper covered in handwriting which she called her fragments; she said she was trying a new approach but wasn't sure if it was working. Morgan found himself missing Savannah's more caustic style; she'd been too busy to attend, apparently, and not even the promise of Gill had tempted her to 'drag her ass' all the way there. He was starting to feel she had a point.

Later, when Eve spread her fragments over a spare bed in their room, he felt he was being kept at bay. She moved the scraps around, as if trying to solve a puzzle, and then began to type frenetically. He retreated to the loft and read a spy thriller he found by the bed. Two chapters in, he knew how it would play out and laid the book aside. He waited until Eve's typing went from fever pitch to intermittent bursts.

"Can I join you down there?" he asked.

"I won't stop you," came the unpromising reply.

He climbed down the ladder and lay next to her on the bed while she worked for another half-hour. When she closed her laptop, he asked if she had brought the silver bell to the retreat. She told him it was too heavy to wear around her neck, so she'd left it at home.

"Don't take offense at that; I love the bell. I've found a place for it in my eyrie."

"That matters a lot."

"*You* matter a lot."

"Do I? I can't always tell. You said we needed to let go of each other…"

"I said for now, not forever."

She joined him under the covers, and when her breathing slowed, he rested his forehead in the shallows of her neck.

The next few days followed a similar pattern. Morgan sat with Eve at meals and check-ins, but the rest of the time they led separate lives. In the evenings, she was tired and disinclined to talk. Morgan made no demands; he did what was needed to avoid being banished from her bed.

It was Robin who offered him a place to lay his story. She found him in the courtyard one evening when she came there for respite from a roommate who snored.

"I can't concentrate on anything," Robin complained. "What's your excuse?"

"Eve and Jess are talking in the room," he said. "They probably haven't even noticed I've left."

She asked how things had been since they last saw each other, and he told her what he had learned about the photograph and the secret of the baby's death. She seemed to understand his mother's need to keep such a traumatic experience hidden.

"Can you talk about this with Eve?" Robin asked.

"You're the only one I've told besides family."

She patted his hand and they sat for a while in companionable silence. When he returned to the room, Eve was alone and said that Jess had left some time ago. She seemed unusually soft and welcoming, and when he joined her in bed and turned on his side, she put her hands in the small of his back. He lay awake a long time wishing he had told Robin about intruding on Eve's private ceremony with Luke. She might have helped him move on and even forgive himself.

They were still physically close when they woke in the morning, and Morgan felt emboldened to stroke the inside of Eve's thigh. But then Jess burst into their room.

"Gill's not coming to the readings anymore," she cried. "Apparently, his publisher double-booked."

When neither of them responded, Jess wailed that no one seemed to care and ran downstairs to find someone who did. The moment for intimacy had passed. They dressed and went down to the main kitchen where the rest of the women had gathered to talk about how they should proceed.

"Does it really make any difference?" Robin asked. "We can go ahead as planned. Isn't the whole point that we've matured as writers?"

Despite her confident claim, the reading session when it came felt flat. Morgan got positive comments on the changes he'd made to his story, but Eve managed to scatter her writing scraps all over the floor. He was helping her gather them up when he was caught off guard by a question from Lily.

"What about you two?" she asked, pointing to them both. "Where do you go from here? We've watched you all week. What happens to your story?"

A silence followed, so protracted that several people shifted uncomfortably in their seats. Eve refused to meet Morgan's gaze and her expression was unreadable.

"We will continue to love each other," Morgan said, into the void.

All eyes turned to Eve, as if he hadn't spoken.

"It's complicated," she said.

Morgan fled the room; he didn't care how foolish he looked. He went up on the same road he had taken with Savannah and half-walked, half-ran until his shirt stuck to his back in salty patches. Eve had hung him out to dry, first with her silence and then with inadequate words.

When his anger cooled, Morgan berated himself for wasting his time and giving too much. Eve had shown exactly how little he meant to her. He would drop her at the cabin, but he wouldn't stay to meet her friends.

He returned to the courtyard, relieved to have made a plan for himself and determined not to suffer any longer. He was surprised to find Jess waiting for him.

"That was horrible," she said. "I'm so sorry. But you need to cut Eve some slack. February is a hard month for Eve. You don't recover easily from that kind of loss."

"I have no idea what you're talking about. I'm this close to walking away, so you'd better tell me."

"She lost a child," Jess said, after a struggle with her conscience. "Stillborn. Two years ago, this month."

Morgan felt his world tilt and then come back into clearer focus. Eve's stiltedness around the topic of children, her work with the dying, the gossamer of grief that clung to her even when she seemed happy. All week he had competed for scraps of her attention, but her focus would have been with the dead child. If only she had trusted him enough to share that burden.

"The piece you read about your mother," Jess continued, "was a little close to the bone. It wasn't that long ago that Eve scattered her dead baby's ashes."

With that, the whole picture came into view: the vase in Eve's sanctuary; the card propped against its base; and of course, the ceremony performed by husband and wife down by the lake.

"But I didn't know," Morgan wailed in anguish.

There was nothing he could say to her now. He wasn't even supposed to know her secret. Jess had given him the burden of knowledge, but with no way of using it for any relief. All he could do was avoid their bedroom and pretend he was being considerate of Eve.

That night, he came late to the final dinner and arrived at the same time as Gill who burst in with an apology and several bottles of champagne.

"I feel terrible about the double-booking," Gill said. "I'm buying your forgiveness."

He opened the first bottle, and when the cork flew up to the ceiling, the women cheered. They toasted their ongoing commitment to writing. Gill stayed long enough to speak with each of them in turn.

"If you don't mind me saying, you look a bit rough," he observed to Morgan. "I hope it's because you are consumed by your craft. Savannah sent me a full copy of her manuscript, by the way. Unsolicited, of course."

"You have to admire her confidence," Morgan said, and then he regaled Gill with stories from his visit.

He laid it on thick about Pinky, and Gill laughed so hard he choked on his drink. When he recovered, he asked Morgan if he'd be willing to repeat the exercise.

"Not the drama, but the dog tending part. I'm going to Boston soon, and my usual dog sitter is away. You didn't meet Beaux, but he's good as gold. It would just be for a week next month."

"I've heard that before," Morgan laughed. "To be honest, I don't think I can take any more time off work."

"Would it sweeten the pie if I agreed to do an interview?"

It would, but he said he had to check with Zoe first. Gill left soon after, and Morgan was about to make his own excuses when Eve commanded the room.

"I was cowardly this morning," she said. "Morgan and I love each other, although I don't think it's anyone's business but ours. But love is complicated; that much is true."

28

The party broke up, but Morgan stayed late to help with dishes. When he guessed Eve would be asleep, he slunk back to the loft. In the morning, he left for breakfast before Eve was awake. When he came back into the room, she was packing.

"I think we should talk," he said.

"You're the one who's been avoiding me."

"I needed space to think - about what you said last night and what you didn't say before. Do you think you were more honest the first time?"

Eve zipped her suitcase, the sound of an angry hornet, and brushed past him to go downstairs. Moments later, Jess appeared and got the rest of Eve's things. When he followed her down, she was loading bags into her car. Eve was in the passenger seat.

"What are you doing?" he asked. "Eve's coming with me."

"Not any more. She went out on a limb for you last night and you ghosted her."

"Please," he begged, opening the car door and talking directly to Eve. "Let's drive to the cabin and talk; I don't need to stay, but we can't end things like this."

She stared at him for a moment; then, without a word, she got out the car. He retrieved her bags and she followed him to the truck. Jess looked furious, but Morgan didn't care. He drove quickly, afraid Eve would change her mind. He drove until the truck was almost out of gas.

In the late afternoon, they bumped down a dirt road and followed Ruby's directions to a cabin set back among trees. They found a note pinned to the door: the women were out walking, but the key was hidden under the mat. It was not as welcoming as the Owl's Nest cabin. The rooms felt dusty and the only bedroom was strewn with clothes.

"I guess we're on the pull-out in the lounge," Eve said. "It could be cozy by the fire."

"More like dark and depressing. Did you see the size of those pines?"

In the kitchen, a set of instructions taped on the fridge looked like something his father would have written. Eve pushed him aside and peered into the fridge. Rows of apple slices spooned like lovers in a pastry tart. She shut the fridge door again with a snap.

Laughter announced the arrival of Ruby and her friend whose name made him think of car tires. She had the merest hint of a Canadian accent. He shook hands with both of them which made Ruby laugh.

For the next few hours, he watched as the women launched multiple conversations and began the mutual task of making dinner. The only time Eve paid him attention was when Micheline produced a bottle of wine. She couldn't find a corkscrew, so Eve asked Morgan to get his Swiss Army knife from the truck. He opened the bottle outside between his knees, and when the cork slid out, he took a slug from the bottle.

"Are you going to share?" Eve asked, from the doorway. "You're being unsociable."

"I was just letting you ladies catch up."

At dinner, Micheline asked how they met, and Eve told

her version of their story. It seemed to make her nostalgic, and she touched his leg under the table.

"How about you two?" Morgan asked, and the women gazed at each other with naked attraction.

"The grocery store," Ruby began.

"We locked eyes," Micheline continued.

"She forgot to give me change."

"I was flustered."

"When she finally did give me change, I noticed she had beautiful hands."

"And you're both married to other people?" he asked. "How do you make that work?"

"Tolerance," Ruby said.

"No one can possess the other," Micheline added. "We have rules. Birthdays and anniversaries are off-limits. We try to be sensitive. Right now, for instance, we're technically visiting friends."

"I envy you," Eve admitted, with a sigh.

Ruby and her lover left mid-morning, but insisted their guests stay longer; Eve could return the key when she was back in town. All they had to do was reverse the instructions on the fridge and leave the place clean.

With their departure, all positivity seemed to leach from the cabin. It began to rain, so Morgan got the fire going and turned on several of the lamps; despite this, there was a pervading sense of gloom.

"I had the craziest dream last night," Eve said, above the crackle of flames. "Anna, my contractor, was in it and we were making love."

Morgan jabbed the fire with a poker.

"She reminds me of you," Eve continued. "There's something in the features. Of course, she doesn't have your beautiful hair."

"I'm thinking of shaving it off," he said, pulling his head away from her hand.

"Don't be moody; it was just a dream. I want to be able to say anything to you, anything at all."

In the afternoon, the rain stopped and they walked out to a waterfall. Morgan wanted to climb to the top, but the rocks were wet and Eve's shoes were flimsy. They stayed low, and he took a series of pictures: Eve bent over a fern; Eve staring off into space; Eve caught in a rainbow.

Later, when evening gathered them in, they lay in each other's arms and dozed. But Eve woke in the middle of a nightmare in which an intruder had breached the cabin. She made him check all the windows and doors.

In the morning, Morgan made eggs and they ate half-dressed, using the bed as a picnic table. When he got up to wash the dishes, Eve followed him out to the kitchen and laid her face on his back.

"I'm sorry," she said. "I wish things were different. Is it too early for a beer?"

They shared a bottle out on the back deck, with Eve naked under a wool blanket.

"Where would you live if you could be anywhere in the world?" she asked.

"I'd keep moving," he said. "I might start in South America and go from there."

"I'd find a valley with woods and a stream. I'd have my own yurt and live on the edge of a community."

"Would I be there?" he asked, swinging his legs over the side of an Adirondack chair.

"Was I in your travel plans?" she countered. "This isn't about you; it's about escaping my history."

She held the beer bottle upside down to show it was empty, so he got up and tried the sliding glass door.

"Did you happen to bring a key with you?" he asked. "Otherwise, I think we're locked out."

"What about a window?" she asked.

"You had me close them after your dream."

It was Eve who noticed the partially open oval window at the tip of the A-frame, and Eve who spied the young man splitting logs. Before Morgan could stop her, she had wandered down the track to ask him for help.

"Jed is coming to our rescue," she said, on her return. "He's gone to fetch a ladder."

Jed was young, strong and nimble; his man-bun bobbed as he shimmied up the ladder in seconds and began to unscrew the window frame. A rip near the seat of his jeans left much of him exposed.

"It's almost indecent," Eve whispered. "Oh, to be that young."

Above them, Jed had removed the window frame, and his firm buttocks hung in the air for a moment before he vanished inside. They could hear him clattering down the stairs. Moments later, he opened the front door.

"That was so...competent," Eve said. "Thank you. How can we repay the kindness?"

"You already have," Jed said, pointing to Eve's blanket which had slipped down a notch.

"Did he really say that?" Morgan asked, when they were alone again.

But Eve thought it was sweet. Now that the emergency was over, she seemed bleak and disinterested. She wanted to pack up and head to town before it got too late. They cleaned with quiet efficiency and took care of everything on the list. As they drove away, Jed waved from outside his cabin; he seemed to be waiting for another damsel in distress.

Miles passed in silence until they stopped for food at a roadside diner. They ate outside, under gas heaters, and drank coffee from the usual thick-lipped mugs.

"Do you think this is working?" Morgan asked. "We neither of us seem happy."

"On bad days, I'm angry at you for falling in love."

29

Back on the road, they used the radio as distraction. When Ruby called to find out how the rest of the weekend had gone, Eve gave vague answers. Then Jess called and pretty soon Eve was crying. Morgan looked straight ahead and pretended not to notice.

"It's almost Valentine's Day," she said, when he dropped her at the airport. "Can you believe that? Promise me that even though it's difficult, you won't walk away."

"I promise," he said.

On Valentine's morning, he sent flowers to her place of work. When she phoned later to thank him, he asked if she was doing anything special. She said it wasn't a great day for ex-partners or long-distance loves. Luke had sent flowers too, but she wasn't reading anything into the gesture; he'd sent some to her mother as well.

"I'm staying in tonight, in case you wondered," Morgan said. "Pizza for one on the couch."

"Such a romantic," Eve teased.

"We could eat together over the phone if you like; I could woo you from afar."

"I'm actually on my way out. I'm meeting Ruby and Micheline at the Red Velvet Lounge. My therapist says it's good for me to come out of seclusion."

"I'll call and wish you goodnight then; what time do you think you'll be home?"

"Not late. I'll be the third wheel."

Morgan called at ten and then again at half-past. Both times, Eve's phone went straight to voicemail. He watched a thriller he had seen before and then he left a message on her phone: he was sorry he had missed her; he hoped she'd had a good time; perhaps next year they could spend Valentine's Day together.

He slept badly. The pizza sat like stone in his stomach and refused to move. There was no call from Eve the next day or the day after that. He left various messages, making his voice sound curious rather than concerned. After a while, he gave up all pretense. With a raised voice, he said he didn't appreciate her disregard. Unless there was a good reason for her silence, she needn't bother contacting him ever again.

That evening, an email message arrived from Eve. Morgan felt such relief he didn't notice the tag line: *I have something to tell you.* The first sentence of the message repeated the same line only with the words *very difficult* inserted in the middle.

He ran various scenarios in his head: she was ending things; she was back with Luke; she needed a break; she had fucked some guy at the Red Velvet Lounge. When he reached the end of the email, he went straight back to the beginning. Then, he swiped his beer off the table with one vicious hand. The bottle bounced but didn't break and liquid that resembled blood pooled on his kitchen floor. He called Eve and she answered on the second ring.

"You must have got my message," she said.

"When - did - this - happen?" he asked, isolating each word, as if it was a specimen.

"Why does that matter?"

"It matters to me. When did you fuck someone else, and who is this lucky person?"

"I'm not going to talk to you if you're going to be like this," Eve said, keeping her voice calm.

"Like this? I'm not the one screwing around."

"I will not point out the irony of that. I'm hanging up. I want to talk to you, but only when you are calm."

The line went dead and Morgan wanted to hurl his phone against the wall; only the cost of it stopped him. He called back immediately, but Eve did not pick up. He called again and again; each time he left a message stating the same questions he had already asked.

When he grew tired of making calls, he re-read Eve's email to see if she had left any clues. She used the word recent: *I was recently physical with someone.* Was that last week? Last month? *I suspect you might feel hurt by this.* No shit, Eve. *You might even feel betrayed.* You think? *It doesn't need to change anything between us.*

"It changes everything," Morgan shouted, into the empty room.

He drank whatever he could find in his apartment which turned out to be two beers and some miniature bottles of Baileys left over from his sister's visit.

"I've always loved Bailey's," Faith said, when he called her, half-drunk. "Don't you remember? I used to sneak bottles into my room."

"You're disgusting."

"When you insult me, I know you're not okay."

"You were right about Eve."

"Oh, Morgan, I'm so sorry. I didn't want to be right. Do you want me to come there? I'd have to find a sitter, cook meals for Jerry in advance, cancel a few meetings."

"Don't do it," he said, "but thank you."

"I knew she was trouble. Hang in there and don't do anything stupid."

"Like get off my face on lighter fluid?"

"No. Like calling her and being an ass."

Morgan read Eve's email one last time. After her main

confession, she had heaped on the bullshit: *I wasn't ready for what you had to offer; I don't deserve you; I never meant to open up to anyone else.*

He retrieved all of Eve's letters and sorted them by date. Then, he read them aloud, like a one-woman show, and threw them into the empty pizza box. On his sliver of a deck, he doused the box in lighter fluid - his joke about huffing had given him the idea.

"To Eve and all who sail in her," he cried, as he struck a match and sent the box up in flames.

The neighbor's patio door slid open, and a man's voice asked if everything was okay. Morgan said it was all under control and the door slid shut. In minutes, Eve's words were reduced to ash. Later, when the remains had cooled, Morgan scooped them into a thick glass jar and placed it on a shelf. When he finally spoke to Eve, he kept the jar in his line of vision.

"I need details," he said. "I need to know how and when it all went wrong."

"Nothing went wrong. This wasn't planned; it just happened – like we happened."

"But we didn't just happen. I was minding my own business at the retreat when you pursued me."

"You can believe what you like; maybe I deserve your cruelty. But trust me, I'm suffering enough."

"I want to know who you slept with," he asked again. "You owe me that much at least."

Like any good interviewer, he knew when to stay quiet. He let the silence stretch, until Eve felt compelled to fill it with a piece of truth. But the revelation brought him no satisfaction, just more pain.

"I'm coming to stay with Jess," Eve said. "She's offered a safe place, away from all the judgement. Could we meet and talk in person? Doors are slamming shut so fast in my life, I feel as if I have emotional whiplash."

"You want me to feel sorry for you?"

"I want you to have a little compassion."

He made no promises. He would let Eve stew in her own juices, as his mother would say. The thought of Margaret brought a spasm of pain. If circumstances had been different, Eve might have helped him understand the experience of losing a child.

With the letters burned, his next task was to clean the truck. He wanted to remove every strand of Eve's hair, every sweet wrapper. After that, he purged his apartment and threw away his Marvel sheets. He crafted what might be his last email to Eve. She had made choices, and he would do the same. He was hurt – the last few months had been hard – but he was willing to meet in the spirit of closure. After that, they would go their separate ways.

Eve replied instantly and tried to change the terms of their meeting. She proposed a night together so they could hold each other as they talked. But Morgan said it was the retreat place or nothing.

He packed like a warrior going into battle: his green canvas bag and writing materials, Gill's book, an envelope with the gifts Eve had given him. Last, but not least, the jar of ashes.

The ferry ride was smooth, and he found he could drive to Gill's house from memory. As he climbed the wooden steps, the front door opened and a portly Labrador lumbered out. Morgan crouched down and Beaux nuzzled into his shoulder.

"He likes you," Gill said. "That was easy. Do you want something to drink? We can talk through Beaux's simple needs."

"Whatever you're having."

"A vile concoction made by my herbalist?"

"Coffee then," Morgan laughed, dropping his bags and checking his appearance in the hall mirror.

"You look better than the last time I saw you," Gill said. "You're pale and a bit skinny, but there is something determined in your face."

"I expected a different kind of dog," Morgan admitted. "Something small and tidy."

"Beaux wasn't my choice, but he's a link to Colin. I'll be a mess when he goes. Enough of that. Let's get down to business."

Beaux would be a synch. He wasn't allowed on beds or sofas, and his only bad habit was rolling on dead fish. With that resolved, they moved on to the interview. Gill wanted to focus on Colin's environmental legacy. In return, he gave unpublished details about his writing life.

"Feel free to use my desk while you're here," Gill said, when they had finished. "And take your heartbreak out to the water. It helps, believe me."

Alone in the house, Morgan found his spots: the sofa near the picture window, the kitchen bar, the desk that was perfect for writing. Eve had sent a message with another proposed change of plan. She wanted him to come into Seattle tomorrow evening. She had a surprise and named a specific time and place to meet. He agreed, partly from exhaustion, noticing that Eve sounded full of confidence and unashamed.

In the afternoon, he took Beaux down to the water and threw tennis balls until his arm ached. They paddled in tide pools and Morgan collected whatever shells drew his fancy. A heron joined them, in search of food, but Beaux ran him off into deeper water.

There was no television in Gill's house, so Morgan went to bed early. He slept badly and woke just as the sun dragged the mountain out of mist. Back on the beach with Beaux, they watched seals bob like ghosts in the water and then heave themselves out to lay on the rocks.

Back at the house, he gave Beaux a bone and set off for the ferry. In his jacket pocket, he carried three diminished treasures. He released the first of them from the back of the boat, and the silver ring disappeared into the water without a trace.

The meet-up spot turned out to be a Mexican restaurant near the college. Eve was already there, dressed in the long green skirt she had worn on the last day of the retreat. She looked serious but not distraught. She had ordered beers along with guacamole and chips.

"I'm sorry I messed up your plan," she said. "If you want, we could go to the retreat place another time."

"There is no other time. After this, we're done."

"You don't mean that," she said, but for the first time she looked uncertain.

"I should have known it was Anna," Morgan said, unable to stop himself. "You'd been telling me, one way or another, for weeks."

"I don't want to talk about her."

"At least tell me how long it has been going on."

"Since the Red Velvet Lounge."

"Valentine's night? How could you do that?"

"We just got talking. There's a sadness in her I understand. None of this was planned. It just…"

"Happened. I know. Are you still seeing her?"

Eve looked down at the table.

"That answers that. Do you love her?"

Eve shook her head; tears began to leak from her eyes, and the couple at the next table looked over. Images of Eve with Anna flooded Morgan's mind: Anna with her practical skills and her enviable tool belt.

When Eve went to the restroom, Morgan set the Buddha emblem and the spinning top by her half-finished beer. But then his phone pinged, and it was her saying she was out on the sidewalk.

"Surprise!" she said, thrusting a ticket into his hand. "It's a recital by that poet we like; she's here for one night only. It was sold out, but Ruby pulled some strings. You won't be able to stay mad when you hear her," she added, with a touch of the old confidence.

On the tree-lined walkway that led to the venue, they

mingled with students and poetry lovers. A young man made a joke, trying to get Eve's attention, and Morgan responded with something crude. Eve laughed, and hooked her arm in his, as if he was her protector.

"There's Ruby," she said, when they got inside. "I'll invite her to sit with us."

"Please don't. This is the last time we are ever going to see each other."

She dropped his arm and went over to her friend. They talked for a few minutes and then embraced.

"I've explained the situation," she said, when she returned. "Ruby understands."

Morgan could not give a fuck. The poet appeared and he forced his mind to concentrate. She was dressed all in black and was almost lost behind the podium. Despite this, she held the crowd rapt. Her poems were uncomplicated jewels. Later, as they walked back through the avenue of trees, Eve asked which poem had been his favorite.

"The last one," he said. "The ending. You do know this is goodbye, right?"

"But we've barely talked. I could stay with you tonight, if you let me. I'm curious to see Gill's place, and we need time to process this."

"There's nothing to process. It was over when you did what you did. We've been circling the drain for weeks."

They had walked the few blocks back to his truck. Eve clung to him, and he was forced to peel her fingers from his arm.

"Aren't you going to hug me?" she asked.

"I think it's better that I don't."

He got into the driver's side of the truck. Before he could close the door, Eve leaned in and kissed him; she left tears on his cheek. He drove away fast, not looking back, and it took him a while to realize he was going in the wrong direction. When he pulled over at a gas station, his hands were shaking.

"I'm sorry, Beaux," he said, when he got back to a mess on the kitchen floor. "Blame human heartbreak."

In the garden, Morgan sat on the steps while Beaux did his business. Then the dog nudged his head under Morgan's hand and drummed a rhythmic beat with his tail. As if invited, Morgan expounded on the perils and pitfalls of human love.

"I ripped off the band-aid, Beaux. I ripped off the band-aid and it hurts like hell."

30

Morgan shaved his head over the basin in the guest bathroom. He used a simple razor, discovered among his toiletries, that may have belonged to either Eve or Kim. It was blunt, reminiscent of his playground assault years earlier, but he still made small cuts as he drew the blade across his head. He had removed his ponytail with scissors, and it lay like a fox's brush on the bathroom tile.

When he was done, Morgan stuck bits of toilet paper on the nicks and stared at himself in the mirror. He looked like a plucked chicken or a child's piñata. But then he thought of the men at the Pueblo who danced their new year into being. He too was crossing a threshold.

Eve had pleaded for another chance then pleaded for at least a conversation. But she had Jess, her therapist, Ruby, Luke, and now Anna. When he remembered Anna, it was easier to hold firm. He had told her to stop calling.

Morgan ran a hand over his head and dislodged the bits of paper. It would be cold down by the water, but he had his woolen hat and he could borrow one of the thick coats that must have belonged to Colin.

"You're staying here, Beaux," he told the dog. "I need to do this alone."

He walked out through the front garden and thought of Gill telling him to value his own story. The first draft version had been full of holes - stray bits dredged up from his unconscious - but now he had a clearer vision. The weeks of infatuation with Eve had played an important part in this harvest. Rejection and betrayal had forced a reckoning with his pain.

At the water's edge, Morgan made a seat out of driftwood and watched the sky grow orange with the sun's first light. He held up the glass jar of ashes. What courage it must have taken to sprinkle the remains of a dead child, he thought. His own offering slipped more easily into the current.

A memory came: his mother in the kitchen canning the last of the year's fruit while his brother stamped winter from his boots by the back door. It was a day when Morgan and Tom had argued over a snowman and he'd sought solace in his room. but later that day, he had looked out of his bedroom window and seen two new shapes in the yard. He'd run down, thrown on a pair of boots, and burst into the yard. Tom had made a mini-snowman with a snow dog at his side.

Love had been all around him, but he hadn't been able to appreciate it back then. He felt exhausted. Eve had turned him inside out, and he had lost himself in her story. It was time to come back to his own sense of self. He had bridges to build, slowly and with care. Hell, he might even go to Kim's wedding; the possibility made him laugh.

Morgan wiped the inside of the jar with his sleeve. As light claimed the sky, he walked back up to the house and sat at Gill's desk to write a letter. He didn't allude to the photograph or the dead child, he simply told his mother that he had been writing stories about his childhood – the pains and the pleasures. He wondered if she would like to read them some time.

Margaret might never acknowledge the letter; she might never read his stories. It didn't matter. She would know of their existence and that would be a link between them. He wondered if it would feel different when they spent time together in the future; he wondered if she would see that some of the fight had left him.

Beaux was asleep at his feet. He rested his hand on the dog's head for a moment and thought about Sideways. Then he smiled and wrote one last poem about Eve. She would never see it, but that didn't matter either. The act of writing carried its own force; the act of writing was enough.

I did not notice you
that is how it began.
In a room thick
with women
I moved among you
like a ghost.
The only man,
a lonely man,
heart like a ship's horn
on a foggy morning,
one brown sock
one blue.
I wish I had listened
really listened
when you placed
your heart
in the circle
for the first time.
I did not notice you
until I ran aground.

ABOUT THE AUTHOR

Julia Doggart is the author of *Return:(Re)membering a Family Life*. She spent many happy years in the US and earned a PhD in Literature from the University of Wisconsin-Madison. She currently lives in Wales where she dreams of getting a dog and works with writers on-line through her website: www.craftedessence.com.

Printed in Great Britain
by Amazon

26729064R00118